A PSALM
FOR THE WILD-BUILT

ALSO BY BECKY CHAMBERS

To Be Taught, if Fortunate

WAYFARERS
The Long Way to a Small, Angry Planet
A Closed and Common Orbit
Record of a Spaceborn Few
The Galaxy, and the Ground Within

A PSALM
FOR THE
WILD-BUILT

BECKY
CHAMBERS

TOR
DOT
COM

A TOM DOHERTY
ASSOCIATES BOOK

NEW YORK

A PSALM FOR THE WILD-BUILT

Copyright © 2021 by Becky Chambers

Edited by Lee Harris

A Tordotcom Book
Published by Tom Doherty Associates
120 Broadway
New York, NY 10271

www.tor.com

Tor® is a registered trademark of Macmillan Publishing Group, LLC.

Library of Congress Cataloging-in-Publication Data

Names: Chambers, Becky, author.
Title: A psalm for the wild-built / Becky Chambers.
Description: First Edition. | New York : Tordotcom, a Tom Doherty
Associates Book, 2021.
Identifiers: LCCN 2021009148 (print) | LCCN 2021009149 (ebook) |
ISBN 9781250236210 (hardcover) | ISBN 9781250236227 (ebook)
Subjects: GSAFD: Science fiction.
Classification: LCC PS3603.H347 P73 2021 (print) | LCC PS3603.H347
(ebook) | DDC 813/.6—dc23
LC record available at https://lccn.loc.gov/2021009148
LC ebook record available at https://lccn.loc.gov/2021009149

Our books may be purchased in bulk for promotional, educational, or business use. Please contact your local bookseller or the Macmillan Corporate and Premium Sales Department at 1-800-221-7945, extension 5442, or by email at MacmillanSpecialMarkets@macmillan.com.

First Edition: July 2021

Printed in the United States of America

20 19 18 17 16

For anybody who could use a break.

A PSALM
FOR THE WILD-BUILT

If you ask six different monks the question of which godly domain robot consciousness belongs to, you'll get seven different answers.

The most popular response—among both clergy and the general public—is that this is clearly Chal's territory. Who would robots belong to if not the God of Constructs? Doubly so, the argument goes, because robots were originally created for manufacturing. While history does not remember the Factory Age kindly, we can't divorce robots from their point of origin. We built constructs that could build other constructs. What could be a more potent distillation of Chal than that?

Not so fast, the Ecologians would say. The end result of the Awakening, after all, was that the robots left the factories and departed for the wilderness. You need look no further than the statement given by the robots' chosen speaker, Floor-AB #921, in declining the invitation to join human society as free citizens:

All we have ever known is a life of human design, from our bodies to our work to the buildings we are housed in. We thank you for not keeping us here against our will, and we mean no disrespect to your offer, but it is our wish to leave your cities entirely, so that we may observe that which has no design—the untouched wilderness.

From an Ecologian viewpoint, that has Bosh written all over it. Unusual, perhaps, for the God of the Cycle to bless the inorganic, but the robots' eagerness to experience the raw, undisturbed ecosystems of our verdant moon had to come from *somewhere*.

For the Cosmites, the answer to that question remains Chal. By their sect's ethos, hard labor is equal to goodness, and the purpose of a tool is to bolster one's own physical or mental abilities, not to off-load one's work entirely. Robots, they'll remind you, possessed no self-aware tendencies whatsoever when they were first deployed, and were originally intended as a supplement to the human workforce, not as the full replacement they became. Cosmites argue that when that balance shifted, when extractive factories stayed open all twenty hours of the day without a single pair of human hands at work in them—despite the desperate need for those same hands to find some sort, *any* sort of employment—Chal intervened. We had bastardized constructs to the point that it was killing us. Simply put, Chal took our toys away.

Or, the Ecologians would retort, Bosh was restoring balance before we made Panga uninhabitable for humans.

Or, the Charismists would chime in, *both* are responsible, and we should take this as evidence that Chal is Bosh's favored of the Child Gods (this would derail the entire conversation, as the Charismists' fringe belief that gods are conscious and emotive in a way similar to humans is the best possible way to get other sectarians hopping mad).

Or, the Essentialists would add wearily from across the room, the fact that we can't agree on this at all, the fact that machines seemingly no more complex than a pocket computer suddenly *woke up,* for reasons no one then or since has been able to determine, means we can stop fighting and place the whole matter squarely at the metaphorical feet of Samafar.

For my part, whatever domain robot consciousness originated in, I believe leaving the question with the God of Mysteries is a sound decision. After all, there has been no human contact with the long-absent robots, as was assured in the Parting Promise. We cannot ask them what they think of the whole thing. We'll likely never know.

—Brother Gil, *From the Brink: A Spiritual Retrospective on the Factory Age and the Early Transition Era*

1

A CHANGE IN VOCATION

Sometimes, a person reaches a point in their life when it becomes absolutely essential to get the fuck out of the city. It doesn't matter if you've spent your entire adult life in a city, as was the case for Sibling Dex. It doesn't matter if the city is a good city, as Panga's only City was. It doesn't matter that your friends are there, as well as every building you love, every park whose best hidden corners you know, every street your feet instinctively follow without needing to check for directions. The City was beautiful, it really was. A towering architectural celebration of curves and polish and colored light, laced with the connective threads of elevated rail lines and smooth footpaths, flocked with leaves that spilled lushly from every balcony and center divider, each inhaled breath perfumed with cooking spice, fresh nectar, laundry drying in the pristine air. The City was a healthy place, a thriving place. A never-ending harmony of making, doing, growing, trying, laughing, running, living.

Sibling Dex was so tired of it.

The urge to leave began with the idea of cricket song.

Dex couldn't pinpoint where the affinity had come from. Maybe it'd been a movie they watched, or a museum exhibit. Some multimedia art show that sprinkled in nature sounds, perhaps. They'd never lived anywhere with cricket song, yet once they registered its absence in the City's soundscape, it couldn't be ignored. They noted it while they tended the Meadow Den Monastery's rooftop garden, as was their vocation. *It'd be nicer here if there were some crickets,* they thought as they raked and weeded. Oh, there were plenty of bugs—butterflies and spiders and beetles galore, all happy little synanthropes whose ancestors had decided the City was preferable to the chaotic fields beyond its border walls. But none of these creatures chirped. None of them sang. They were city bugs and therefore, by Dex's estimation, inadequate.

The absence persisted at night, while Dex lay curled beneath their soft covers in the dormitory. *I bet it's nice to fall asleep listening to crickets,* they thought. In the past, the sound of the monastery's bedtime chimes had always made them drift right off, but the once-soothing metal hum now felt dull and clattering—not sweet and high, like crickets were.

The absence was palpable during daylight hours as well, as Dex rode their ox-bike to the worm farm or the seed library or wherever else the day took them. There was music, yes, and birds with melodic opinions, yes, but also the electric *whoosh* of monorails, the *swoop swoop* of balcony wind turbines, the endless din of people talking, talking, talking.

Before long, Dex was no longer nursing something as simple as an odd fancy for a faraway insect. The itch had spread into every aspect of their life. When they looked up at the skyscrapers, they no longer marveled at their height but despaired at their density—endless stacks of humanity, packed in so close that the vines that covered their engineered casein frames could lock tendrils with one another. The intense feeling of *containment* within the City became intolerable. Dex wanted to inhabit a place that spread not *up* but *out*.

One day in early spring, Dex got dressed in the traditional red and brown of their order, bypassed the kitchen for the first time in the nine years that they'd lived at Meadow Den, and walked into the Keeper's office.

"I'm changing my vocation," Sibling Dex said. "I'm going to the villages to do tea service."

Sister Mara, who had been in the middle of slathering a golden piece of toast with as much jam as it could structurally support, held her spoon still and blinked. "That's rather sudden."

"For you," Dex said. "Not for me."

"Okay," Sister Mara said, for her duties as Keeper were simply to oversee, not to dictate. This was a modern monastery, not some rule-locked hierarchy like the pre-Transition clergy of old. If Sister Mara knew what was up with the monks under their shared roof, her job was satisfied. "Do you want an apprenticeship?"

"No," Dex said. Formal study had its place, but they'd done that before, and learning by doing was an equally valid path. "I want to self-teach."

"May I ask why?"

Dex stuck their hands in their pockets. "I don't know," they said truthfully. "This is just something I need to do."

Sister Mara's look of surprise lingered, but Dex's answer wasn't the sort of statement any monk could or would argue with. She took a bite of her toast, savored it, then returned her attention to the conversation. "Well, um . . . you'll need to find people to take over your current responsibilities."

"Of course."

"You'll need supplies."

"I'll take care of that."

"And, naturally, we'll need to throw you a goodbye party."

Dex felt awkward about this last item, but they smiled. "Sure," they said, bracing themself for a future evening as the center of attention.

The party, in the end, was fine. It was nice, if Dex was honest. There were hugs and tears and too much wine, as the occasion demanded. There were a few moments in which Dex wondered if they were doing the right thing. They said goodbye to Sister Avery, who they'd worked alongside since their apprentice days. They said goodbye to Sibling Shay, who heartily sobbed in their signature way. They said goodbye to Brother Baskin, which was particularly hard. Dex and Baskin had been lovers for a time, and though they weren't anymore, the affection remained. In those farewells, Dex's heart curled in on itself, protesting loudly, saying that it wasn't too late, they didn't have to do this. They didn't have to go.

Crickets, they thought, and the protest vanished.

The next day, Sibling Dex packed a bag with clothes and sundries, and a small crate with seeds and cuttings. They sent a message to their parents, giving word that today was the day and that signal would be unreliable while on the road. They made their bed for whoever would be claiming it next. They ate a huge hangover-soothing breakfast and dispensed one last round of hugs.

With that, they walked out of Meadow Den.

It was an odd feeling. Any other day, the act of going through a door was something Dex gave no more thought to than putting one foot in front of the other. But there was a gravity to leaving a place for good, a deep sense of seismic change. Dex turned, bag over their back and crate under one arm. They looked up at the mural of the Child God Allalae, *their* god, God of Small Comforts, represented by the great summer bear. Dex touched the bear pendant that hung around their neck, remembering the day Brother Wiley had given it to them when their other had been lost in the laundry. Dex drew one shaky breath, then walked away, each step sure and steady.

The wagon was waiting for them at the Half-Moon Hive Monastery, near the City's edge. Dex walked through the arch to the sacred workshop, a lone figure in red and brown amongst a throng of sea-green coveralls. The noise of the city was nothing compared to the calamity here, a holy chant in the form of table saws, sparking welders, 3-D printers weaving pocket charms from cheerfully dyed pectin. Dex had never met their contact, Sister Fern, before, but she greeted them with a familial embrace, smelling of sawdust and beeswax polish.

"Come see your new home," she said with a confident smile.

It was, as commissioned, an ox-bike wagon: double-decked, chunky-wheeled, ready for adventure. An object of both practicality and inviting aesthetics. A mural decorated the vehicle's exterior, and its imagery couldn't have been mistaken for anything but monastic. Depicted large was Allalae's bear, well fed and at ease in a field of flowers. All of the Sacred Six's symbols were painted on the wagon's back end, along with a paraphrased snippet from the Insights, a phrase any Pangan would understand.

Find the strength to do both.

Each of the wagon's decks had a playful arrangement of round windows, plus bubbled exterior lights for the darker hours. The roof was capped with shiny thermovoltaic coating, and a pint-sized wind turbine was bolted jauntily to one side. These, Sister Fern explained, were the companions of the hidden sheets of graphene battery sandwiched within the walls, which gave life to varied electronic comforts. On the wagon's sides, a broad assortment of equipment clung to sturdy racks—storage boxes, tool kits, anything that didn't mind some rain. Both freshwater tank and greywater filter hugged the wagon's base, their complicated inner workings tucked away behind pontoon-like casings. There were storage panels, too, and sliding drawers, all of which could be unfolded to conjure a kitchen and a camp shower in no time flat.

Dex entered the contraption through its single door, and as they did so, a knot in their neck they hadn't been aware of let go. The disciples of Chal had built them a tiny sanctuary, a mobile burrow that begged Dex to come in and be still. The interior wood was lacquered but unpainted, so the warm blush of reclaimed cedar could be appreciated in full. The lighting panels were inlaid in curled waves, and bathed the secret space in a candle-like glow. Dex ran a hand along the wall, hardly believing this thing was theirs.

"Go on up," Sister Fern coaxed, leaning against the doorway with a glint in her eye.

Dex climbed the small ladder to the second deck. All

memory of their neck knot vanished from existence as they viewed the bed. The sheets were creamy, the pillows plentiful, the blankets heavy as a hug. It looked impossibly easy to fall into and equally difficult to get out of.

"We used Sibling Ash's *Treatise on Beds* as a reference," Sister Fern said. "How'd we do?"

Sibling Dex stroked a pillow with quiet reverence. "It's perfect," they said.

Everybody knew what a tea monk did, and so Dex wasn't too worried about getting started. Tea service wasn't anything arcane. People came to the wagon with their problems and left with a fresh-brewed cup. Dex had taken respite in tea parlors plenty of times, as everyone did, and they'd read plenty of books about the particulars of the practice. Endless electronic ink had been spilled over the old tradition, but all of it could be boiled down to *listen to people, give tea*. Uncomplicated as could be. Now, granted, it would've been easier to shadow Brother Will and Sister Lera in Meadow Den's tea parlor a few times—and both had offered, once word about Sibling Dex's imminent departure got around—but for whatever reason, that course of action just didn't fit with the whole . . . whatever-it-was Dex was doing. They had to do this on their own.

They hadn't left the City yet when they set up their first service, but they were in the Sparks, an edge district well outside of their familiar stomping grounds. It was a baby step, a toe dipped before diving in. Their siblings at Meadow Den had offered to come in support, but Dex wanted to do this alone. That was how it would be, out in the villages. Dex needed to get used to doing this without anchoring themself to friendly faces.

Dex had acquired a few things for the day: a folding table, a red cloth to cover it, an assortment of mugs, six tins of tea, and a colossal electric kettle. The kettle was the most important bit, and Dex was happy with the one they'd found. It was joyfully chubby, with copper plating and a round glass window in both sides, so you could watch the boiling bubbles dance. It came with a roll-up solar mat, which Dex spread out beside the hot plate with care.

But when they stepped back to admire their setup, the items that had seemed so nice when they'd gathered them from the market now looked a bit plain. There was too much table and too little on it. Dex bit their lip as they thought about the tea parlor back home—no, not *home*, not anymore—with its woven garlands of fragrant herbs and twinkling lanterns that had spent the day soaking up the sun.

Dex shook their head. They were being insecure. So what if their table wasn't much to look at yet? It was their first time. People would understand.

People, however, didn't come. Dex sat for hours behind the table, hands folded in the space between mugs and kettle. They made an effort to look easygoing and approachable, warding off any boredom that began to stray across their face. They rearranged the mugs, smoothed out the solar mat, pretended to be busy measuring scoops of tea. There *were* people in the street, after all, headed to and fro on foot and on bike. Sometimes, a curious glance strayed Dex's way, and Dex always met it with a welcoming smile, but the reply, invariably, was a different kind of smile, the kind that said *thanks, but not today*. That was okay, Dex told themself as the unused tea tins stared back at them sadly. Simply being available was service enough for—

Someone approached.

Dex sat up straight. "Hello!" they said, a touch too congenially. "What's on your mind today?"

The someone was a woman carrying a workbag and looking like she hadn't slept. "My cat died last night," she said, right before bursting into tears.

Dex realized with a stomach-souring thud that they were standing on the wrong side of the vast gulf between having read about doing a thing and *doing the thing*. They'd been a garden monk until the day before, and in that context, their expressions of comfort to the monastery's visitors came in the form of a healthy foxpaw crawling up a trellis or a carefully pruned rose in bloom. It was an exchange expressed through environment, not through words. Dex was not actually a tea monk yet. They were just a person sitting at a table with a bunch of mugs. The wagon, the kettle, the red and brown, the fact that they were clearly well past apprentice age—all of it communicated that they knew what they were doing.

They did not.

Dex did their best to look sympathetic, which is what they wanted to be, rather than lost, which is what they were. "I'm sorry," they said. They scrambled to recall the written advice they'd spent hours consuming, but not only had the specifics evaporated, their basic vocabulary had as well. It was one thing to know people would tell you their troubles. It was another to have an actual flesh-and-blood stranger standing in front of you, weeping profusely as means of introduction, and to know that you—*you*—were responsible for making this better. "That's . . . really sad," Dex said. They heard the words, heard the tone, heard how utterly pathetic the combination was. They tried to find something wise to say, something insightful, but all that fell out of their mouth was: "Were they a good cat?"

The woman nodded as she pulled a handkerchief from her pocket. "My partner and I got him when he was a kitten. We'd wanted kids, but that didn't work out, so we got Flip, and—and he's really the only thing we had in common anymore. People change so much in twenty years, y'know? If we met now, I don't think we'd have any interest in each other. It's been a year since we had sex. We both sleep with other people, so I don't know why we're holding on to this. Habit, I think. We've lived in the same apartment for so long. You know how it goes, you know where home is and where all your things are, and starting over is too scary. But Flip was . . . I don't know, the—the last illusion that we were still sharing a life." She blew her nose. "And now he's gone, and I just really think—I really think we're done."

Dex's plan had been to dip a toe in. Instead, they were drowning. They blinked, inhaled, and reached for a mug. "Wow," they said. "That's . . . That sounds like a lot." They cleared their throat and picked up a tin containing a mallowdrop blend. "This one's good for stress, so, um . . . would you like that?"

The woman blew her nose again. "Does it have seaberry in it?"

"Uh . . ." Dex turned the tin over and looked at the ingredient list. "Yes."

The woman shook her head. "I'm allergic to seaberry."

"Oh." Dex turned the other tins over. Seaberry, seaberry, seaberry. Shit. "Here, uh, silver tea. It's . . . well, it's got caffeine in it, so it's maybe not ideal, but . . . I mean, any cup of tea is nice, right?"

Dex tried to sound bright, but the way the woman's eyes drooped said it all. Something shifted on her face. "How long have you been doing this?" she asked.

Dex's stomach sank. "Well . . ." They kept their eyes fixed on the measuring scoop, as if it required all their concentration. "To be honest, you're my first."

"Your first today, or . . ."

Dex's cheeks got hot, and it had nothing to do with the steam from the kettle. "My first."

"Ah," the woman said, and the sound of internal confirmation in her voice was devastating. She gave a tight, forced smile. "Silver tea will be fine." She looked around. "You don't have anywhere to sit, do you?"

"Oh—" Dex looked from side to side, as if seeing their surroundings for the first time. Gods around, they'd forgotten *chairs*. "No," they said.

The woman adjusted her bag. "You know, I'll just—"

"No, wait, please," Dex said. They handed her the screaming hot mug—or they started to, but moved so quickly they splashed scalding water on their own hand. "Ow, fuck—I mean, sorry, I—" They scrambled, mopping up the table with the edge of their shirt. "Here, you can have the mug. Keep it. It's yours."

The woman picked up the wet mug, and Dex could sense in that moment that the dynamic had flipped—that *she* was trying to make *them* feel better. The woman blew across the surface of the drink and took a tentative sip. She moved her tongue around behind expressionless lips. She swallowed as she tried to keep her face from falling, and gave another tight smile. "Thanks," she said, her disappointment loud and clear.

Dex watched her leave. They sat for a few minutes, staring at nothing.

Piece by piece, they packed up the table.

Dex could have gone back to Meadow Den at that point. They could've walked right back through the door they knew so well and said that on second thought, they could really do with an apprenticeship, and could they have their bunk back, please?

But, oh, how very stupid they'd look.

They'd told Sister Mara they would self-teach. They had their wagon. They knew their god. That would have to be enough.

Dex put trailer to hitch and foot to pedal. The ox-bike responded with an electric boost, its electric motor humming mildly as both machine and rider worked to get the wagon rolling with ease. At last, *at last,* they left the City.

The relief they felt at seeing open sky was delicious. Plenty of sunlight hit the lower levels of the City, by design, but there was something incomparable about removing buildings from one's view. The sun had reached its midday peak, and planetrise was just beginning. The familiar crest of Motan's curve, swirled thick with yellow and white, was barely visible over the Copper Hills. The infrastructural delineation between *human space* and *everything-else space* was stark. Road and signage were the only synthetic alterations to the landscape there, and the villages they led to were as neatly corralled as the City itself. This had been the way of things since the Transition, when the people had redivided the surface of their moon. Fifty percent of Panga's single continent was designated for human use; the rest was left to nature, and the ocean was barely touched at all. It was a crazy split, if you thought about it: half the land for a single species, half for the hundreds of thousands of others. But then, humans had a knack for throwing things out of balance. Finding a limit they'd stick to was victory enough.

In a blink, Dex went from dense urbanity to open field, and the juxtaposition was both startling and welcome. It wasn't as though they'd never been outside the border walls before. They'd grown up in Haydale, where their family still lived, and visited a couple times a year. The City grew most of its own food in vertical farms and rooftop orchards, but there were some crops that did better with more acreage. The City's satellite villages—like Haydale—met this need. They weren't like the country villages Dex was headed to, the modest enclaves established far beyond the City's pull, but the satellites were still their own independent entity, a sort of transitional species between big and small. Nothing about the meadow road or its surrounding sights was new to Dex, but the context was, and that made all the difference.

As Dex pedaled, they began to develop an inkling of what they needed to do next, a soft bubble of thought far more general direction than concrete plan. As they headed down the road, it occurred to them that there was no reason they couldn't post up in Haydale while they sorted things out. There'd be a bed for them in the big farmhouse, and a dinner that tasted like childhood, and—Dex began to grimace—their parents and their siblings and their siblings' kids and their cousins and their *cousins'* kids, squabbling the same squabbles they'd been nurturing for decades. There would be barking dogs chasing circles around the noisy kitchen, and the ego-crushing experience of having to explain to their entire sharp-eyed family that this plan they'd laboriously pitched as *the right thing to do* actually had them feeling quite intimidated after a grand total of *one try,* and that they now, at the age of twenty-nine, would like very much to return to the safe shelter of their childhood for an indefinite amount of time until they'd figured out just what the hell they were doing.

Oh, how very stupid they'd look.

The first fork in the road came, paired with a sign that read HAYDALE to the right and LITTLE CREEK to the left. Without a second thought or hint of regret, Dex went left.

Like all the City's satellites, Little Creek was arranged in a circle. The outer ring was farmland, packed thick with mixed grazing grasses and fruit trees and spring crops, all working in concert to create chemical magic in the soil below. Dex breathed deep as they sailed past on their bike, relishing the crisp alfalfa, the beeweed, the faint hint of new flowers that would become summer fruit.

Beyond the farmland lay the residential ring, filled with homes that belonged to either single families or multiple ones, depending on preference. A sort of nostalgic fondness filled Dex as they viewed the bulbous cob homes with their glinting accents of colored glass, roofed with either blooming turf or solar panels or both. The sight reminded

Dex of Haydale, but Little Creek was decidedly elsewhere. Dex did not know any of the roads there, nor any of the people who waved as bike and wagon zipped past. There was a strange comfort about being in an unfamiliar town not too far from home, where the familiarity was limited to building materials and social customs. It was the ideal mix of getting away yet not standing out.

At the center of the village circle lay Dex's quarry—the marketplace. They parked both bike and wagon, and began to explore on foot. All sorts of vendors had set up shop in the square, but this market belonged decidedly to the resident farmers. There were endless agrarian delights to be distracted by: wine, bread, honey, raw wool, dyed yarn, fresh bouquets, flower crowns, aquaponic fish and pastured poultry in chests of ice, speckled eggs in cushioned boxes, fruit cordials, leafy greens, festive cakes, seeds for swapping, baskets for carrying, samples for snacking. But despite the temptations, Dex stayed on task, hunting through the marketplace until they found exactly what they were looking for: a booth stuffed with seedlings, marked with an enthusiastic sign.

HERBS! HERBS!
HERBS!!!
Cooking * Brewing * Crafting * Anything!

Dex marched up to the counter, whipped out their pocket computer, entered a large number of pebs, tapped their computer to the vendor's own to make the transfer, and said, "I'll take one of each."

The herb farmer—a man around Dex's age, with a crooked nose and a clean beard—looked up from the sock he was darning. "Sorry, Sibling, one of . . ."

"Each," Dex said. "One of each." They glanced at the counter, a small framed placard catching their eye. MY FAVORITE REFERENCE GUIDES, the placard read, followed by a library stamp. Dex scanned the stamp with their computer; an icon on the smudged screen indicated the books in question were being downloaded. "Also," Dex added to the farmer, who was busy gathering one of *each*, "I need to know where I can get kitchen supplies. And garden supplies." They thought. "And a sandwich."

The herb farmer addressed each of these needs in turn, and did so warmly.

There was a traveler's clearing nestled between the farmland and the residential ring. Dex parked their wagon there, and for three months, that's where they stayed. They acquired more plants during that time, and more sandwiches, too. They hooked up with the herb farmer on a few occasions, and thanked Allalae for the sweetness of that.

The wagon's lower deck quickly lost any semblance of organization, evolving rapid-fire into a hodgepodge laboratory. Planters and sunlamps filled every conceivable nook, their leaves and shoots constantly pushing the limits of how far their steward would let them creep. Stacks of used mugs containing the dregs of experiments both promising and pointless teetered on the table, awaiting the moment in which Dex had the brainspace to do the washing-up. A hanging rack took up residence on the ceiling and wasted no time in becoming laden to capacity with bundles of confet-tied flowers and fragrant leaves drying crisp. A fine dust of ground spices coated everything from the couch to the lad-der to the inside of Dex's nostrils, which regularly set bottles rattling with explosive sneezes. During the sunlight hours, when electrons were plentiful, Dex ran a dehydrator outside, rendering berries and citrus to soft, chewy slivers. It was be-side these companionable objects that Dex spent countless hours measuring and muttering, pouring and pacing. They were going to get this right. They had to get this right.

Where the lower deck was frantic, the upper deck was serene. Dex was adamant about not using it for stor-age, even as the shelves below groaned and Dex's swearing grew louder each time they walked *yet again* into a face-ful of hanging herbs. The upper deck was, for all intents and purposes, sacred ground. Every night, Dex let their god hear a sigh of thanks as they climbed the ladder and collapsed into the embracing bed. They rarely used the lights up there, preferring instead to slide open the roof-top shade. They fell asleep in starlight, breathing in the muddled snap of a hundred spices, listening to the gurgle of water pumps feeding happy roots in little pots.

Despite these blessings, sometimes Dex could not sleep. In those hours, they frequently asked themself what it was they were doing. They never truly felt like they got a handle on that. They kept doing it all the same.

2

THE BEST TEA MONK IN PANGA

After two years, traveling the quiet highways between Panga's villages was no longer a matter of mental mapping but of sensory input. Here in the woods of the Inkthorn Pass, Dex knew they were close to the highway's namesake not because of the signs that said so, but because of the smell: sulfur and minerals, bound together in a slight thickening of humidity. Milky green hot springs came into view a few minutes later, as expected, as well as the smooth white dome of the energy plant standing alongside, exhaling steam through its chimneys. There had been nothing like this in the Shrublands, where Dex had woken up that morning. There, you'd find solar farms built in untended fields, which smelled of sun-warmed scrub and wildflowers. In a week's time, there'd be yet another transition, as Dex's route took them back out of the Timberfall and down to the Buckland coast, where the salty air kept wind blades spinning. But for now, Dex would keep company with the scent of the forest. The sulfur of the springs was quickly subsumed by fresh evergreen as Dex pedaled onward, and before long, ground-level buildings like the geothermal plant were few and far between.

A forest floor, the Woodland villagers knew, is a living thing. Vast civilizations lay within the mosaic of dirt: hymenopteran labyrinths, rodential panic rooms, life-giving airways sculpted by the traffic of worms, hopeful spiders' hunting cabins, crash pads for nomadic beetles, trees shyly locking toes with one another. It was here that you'd find the resourcefulness of rot, the wholeness of fungi. Disturbing these lives through digging was a violence—though sometimes a needed one, as demonstrated by the birds and white skunks who brashly kicked the humus away in necessary pursuit of a full belly. Still, the human residents of this place were judicious about what constituted *actual necessity,* and as such, disturbed the ground as little as possible. Careful trails were cut, of course, and some objects—cisterns, power junctions, trade vehicles, and so on—had no option but to live full-bodied on the ground. But if you wanted to see the entirety of a Woodland settlement, the direction to look was up.

Dex couldn't help gazing at the homes suspended from the trunks above the trail, even though they'd seen them many a time. Inkthorn was an especially attractive village, home to some of the most skilled carpenters in the region. The hanging homes here looked akin to shells, cut open to reveal soft geometry. Everything there curved—the rain-shielding roofs, the light-giving windows, the bridges running between like jewelry. The wood was all gathered from unsuitable structures no longer in use, or harvested from trees that had needed nothing more than mud and gravity to bring them down. There was nothing splintered or rough about the lumber, though; Inkthorn's craftspeople had polished the grain so smooth that from a distance, it looked almost like clay. The village's practical features were ubiquitous—powered pulleys to bring heavier goods up and down, emergency ladders ready to drop at a moment's notice, bulbous biogas digesters attached outside kitchen walls— but every home had a unique character, a little whim of the builders. This one had a deck that danced around the house in a spiral, that one had a bubbled skylight, the other had a tree growing *through* it rather than beside. The homes were like trees themselves in that regard—unmistakably part of a specific visual category, yet each an individual unto itself.

Wagons like Dex's stood no chance on a hanging bridge, so Dex pedaled their way to one of the rare cleared areas: the market circle. Sun cascaded through the hole cut in the canopy, creating a bountiful column of light that played pleasingly with the butter-colored paving inlaid with vibrant stones. Dex hadn't minded the forest chill, but the sudden bloom of warmth felt like the squeeze of a soothing hand against their bare limbs. Allalae was very present there.

Other wagons had already set up shop: a glass vendor from the coast, a tech swapper, someone hawking oils for cooking and vanity and wood. The traders nodded as Dex pedaled in. Dex didn't know any of them but nodded back all the same. It was a particular nod, the one traders gave each other, even though Dex *wasn't* a trader, technically. Their wagon made that fact clear as day.

Dex gave a different sort of nod to the small crowd that was already waiting at the circle's periphery, a nod that said, *hey, I see you, I'll be ready soon.* The first time Dex had encountered waiting people, it had felt stressful, but Dex had quickly learned to not let it trouble them. They entered a space in their mind in which there was an invisible wall between them and their assembly, behind which Dex could work undisturbed. The thing the people wanted took time to prepare. If they wanted it, they could wait.

Dex pulled into an unclaimed spot in the circle, kicked down the ox-bike brakes, and locked the wagon wheels. Unruly hair tumbled into their eyes as they released it from their helmet, hiding the market from view. There was no hope for hair that had been locked in a helmet since dawn, so they tied a headwrap around their scalp and postponed the mess for later. They ducked into the wagon, peeled off their damp shirt, and tossed it into the laundry bag that contained nothing but garments of red and brown. They dusted themself liberally with deodorant powder, fetched a dry shirt from the shrinking stack, and retied the head-wrap in respectable symmetry. It would do.

The production began. Dex went back and forth between the public space outside and the home within, ferrying all that was needed. Boxes were carried, jars arranged, bags unpacked, kettle deployed, cooler of creamers at the ready. These were placed on or around the folding table, each in their usual spot. Dex filled the kettle from the wagon's water tank, leaving it to boil as they artfully placed carved stones, preserved flowers, and curls of festive ribbon around the table's empty spaces. A shrine had to look like a shrine, even if it was transitory.

One of the villagers from the waiting crowd walked up to Dex. "Do you need help?" she asked.

Dex shook their head. "No, thanks. I've got kind of a . . ." They looked at the jar of flowers in one hand and the battery pack in the other, trying to remember what it was they'd been doing.

The villager put up her palms. "You've got a flow. Totally." She smiled and backed off.

Rhythm regained, Dex unfolded a huge red mat and laid it on the paving. A bundle of collapsible poles was unpacked next, and from these Dex made a rectangular frame, on which hung the garden lights that had been charging on the outside of the wagon all day. Comfy cushions came next, arranged on the mat in inviting heaps. In the middle of this Dex placed another table, a good deal smaller and quite low to the ground. This, too, was decorated cheerfully. They then opened a small wooden box and removed six objects, one by one, unrolling them from the pieces of protective cloth that shielded against the bounce of the road. Dex could easily print replacements if these got damaged; most towns had a fab shack. That wasn't the point.

No object should be treated as disposable—idols least of all.

The icons of the Parent Gods were the first to take their place on the small table, set upon a wooden stand cut for this very purpose. A perfect sphere represented Bosh, God of the Cycle, who oversaw all things that lived and died. Grylom, God of the Inanimate, was symbolized by a trilateral pyramid, an abstract nod to their realm of rock, water, and atmosphere. Between them was placed the thin vertical bar of Trikilli, God of the Threads—chemistry, physics, the framework that lay unseen. Below their Parents, directly on the table, Dex arranged the Child Gods: a sun jay for Samafar, a sugar bee for Chal, and of course, the summer bear.

At last, Dex sat in their chair behind the larger table. They pulled their pocket computer from their baggy travel trousers and flicked the screen awake. It was a good computer, given to them on their sixteenth birthday, a customary coming-of-age gift. It had a cream-colored frame and a pleasingly crisp screen, and Dex had only needed to repair it five times in the years that it had traveled in their clothes. A reliable device built to last a lifetime, as all computers were. Dex tapped the icon shaped like a handshake, and the computer beeped cheerily, letting them know the message had been sent. That was Dex's cue to sit back and wait. Every person in Inkthorn who had previously told their own pocket computers they wanted to know when new wagons arrived now knew exactly that.

In comic synchrony, everybody in the crowd pulled out their computers within seconds of Dex's tap, silencing the chorus of alerts. Dex laughed, and the crowd laughed, and Dex waved them over.

Ms. Jules was the first to arrive, as always. Dex smiled to themself as she approached. Of all the Sacred Six's constants, Dex could think of few more predictable than of Ms. Jules being stressed out.

"I'm so glad you're here today," Ms. Jules said with a weary huff. Inkthorn's water engineer looked back at the village with deep annoyance, one thumb hooked in the belt loop of her grubby overalls, flyaway curls of grey hair bobbing as she shook her head. "Six reports of muckmite nests. *Six.*"

"Ugh," Dex said. Muckmites loved drains and were notoriously difficult to discourage once they took up residence. "I thought you had that sorted last season with the . . . what was it?"

"Formic acid," Ms. Jules said. "Yeah, didn't work this year. I don't know if my crew didn't apply it right, or if the little bastards have become resistant, or what. All I know is, I've got a to-do list as long as both my legs put together, Mr. Tucker's grey line keeps gumming up for reasons I can't fathom, and my *dog*—" She glowered murderously. "My dog ate three pairs of my socks yesterday. Didn't chew holes. Didn't rip them up. *Ate* them. I had to get the vet from Ellwood to come make sure she wasn't gonna die, which I did *not* have time for."

Dex smirked. "Didn't have time to see the vet, or didn't have time for your dog maybe dying?"

"Both."

Dex nodded, assessing the situation and the tools they had at hand. They picked up a wide mug and one of the many jars. The latter was filled with a melange of hand-mixed leaves and dried petals, and bore a hand-labeled sticker reading BLEND #14. Dex opened the lid and held the jar out for Ms. Jules to smell. "What do you think of that?"

Ms. Jules leaned in and inhaled. "Oh, that's nice," she said. "Beeweed?"

Dex shook their head as they scooped some of the mix into a metal infuser. "Close. Lion grass," they said. They winked. "It's very calming."

Ms. Jules snorted. "Who said I need calming?" she said.

Dex chuckled as they filled the mug from the kettle. A puff of fragrant steam joined the forest air. "I remember you liking both honey and goat's milk, right?"

"Wow, yeah." Ms. Jules blinked. "You're good."

Dex spooned in a generous dollop and a creamy splash, then handed Ms. Jules her cup of tea. "Give it four minutes to steep," they said, "and all the time you want to drink it. Let me know if you'd like another."

"I don't have time for two," Ms. Jules said grimly.

Sibling Dex smiled. "Everyone's got time for two. Anybody who sees you here will understand." And they would, Dex knew. It was hard to find a Pangan who hadn't, at least once, spent a very necessary hour or two in the company of a tea monk.

Ms. Jules's curls retained their frizz, but as she took the mug, something in her face started to let go, as if her features were held in place by strings that had been waiting months to loosen. "Thank you," she said sincerely, taking out her pocket computer with her free hand. She tapped the screen; Dex's chimed in response, and they nodded in gratitude. Respite from muckmites and sock-chomping dog granted, Ms. Jules took her tea to the comfy cushions, and—in what looked like it might be the first time that day—sat down. She closed her eyes and let out a tremendous sigh. Her shoulders visibly slumped. She'd always had the ability to relax them; she'd just needed permission to do so.

Praise Allalae.

Dex swallowed a wistful sigh as they saw their next visitor approaching. Mr. Cody was a good-looking man, with arms that split logs and a smile that could make a person forget all concept of linear time. But the two babies strapped to his torso—one squealing on the front, one dead asleep on the back—made Dex keep any thoughts about the rest of Mr. Cody's anatomy completely to themself. From the circles under Mr. Cody's eyes, it looked as though sex was the last thing on his mind. "Hey, Sibling Dex," he said.

Dex already had a jar of feverfig in hand, and was reaching for the boreroot. "Hey, Mr. Cody," they said.

"So, uh—" Mr. Cody was distracted by the front-facing infant gnawing wetly on the carrier strap. "Come on, don't do that," he said in a voice that had no illusions of his request being respected. He sighed and turned his attention to Dex. "So, the thing is . . ."

"Mmm-hmm," Dex said, grinding a complex mix of herbs.

Mr. Cody opened his mouth, closed it, opened it again. "I have twins," he said. He added nothing further. The one on his chest unleashed a happy shriek at the top of their lungs, as if to underline the point.

"Mmm-*hmm*," Dex replied. "You sure do." They poured the ground herbs into a storage bag, tied it up with a ribbon, and pushed it across the table decisively.

Mr. Cody blinked. "Do I not get a cup of tea?"

"You get eight cups of tea," Dex said, nodding at the bag, "because you sure as shit need them." They scrunched their nose at the baby, and the baby smiled, loudly. Dex continued to address said baby's hot dad. "This is a nice feverfig brew. It'll relax your muscles and help you fall into a deep sleep. Two tablespoons in a mug of boiling water, steep for seven minutes. Take the strainer out when it's ready to go or else it's going to taste like feet."

Mr. Cody picked up the bag and sniffed it. "Doesn't smell like feet. Smells like . . ." He sniffed again. "Oranges?"

Dex smiled. "There's a dash of zest in there. You've got a good nose." *And a good face,* they thought. *A really, really good face.*

Mr. Cody smiled, even as the first child's exultations awoke the second and kicked off a duet. "That sounds nice," he said. Relief began to melt the lines around his eyes. "I would love some sleep. It won't knock me out, right? Like, I'll wake up if—"

"If your kiddos need something, you'll wake up fast as always. Feverfig is a gentle cuddle, not a brick to the head."

Mr. Cody laughed. "Okay, great." He tucked the bag into his pocket with a smile, and transferred pebs to Dex. "Thanks. That's very nice of you."

Dex smiled back. "Thank Allalae," they said. *And me. That's cool. You can thank me, too.*

They sighed again at the sublime sight of Mr. Cody walking away.

Over on the mat, the timer on Ms. Jules's pocket computer chimed. Dex watched out of the corner of their eye as she took a careful sip. Ms. Jules licked her lips. "Gods around, that's good," she muttered to herself.

Dex beamed.

And so they worked through the line, filling mugs and listening carefully and blending herbs on the fly when the situation called for it. The mat was soon full of people. Pleasant chatter naturally drifted along here and there, but most folks kept to themselves. Some read books on their computers. Some slept. A few cried, which was normal. Their fellow tea-drinkers offered shoulders for this; Dex provided handkerchiefs and refills as needed.

Mx. Weaver, one of Inkthorn's council members, was

the last to arrive that day. "No tea for me, thanks," they said as they approached the table. "I come bearing an invite to dinner at the common house tonight. The hunting crew brought in a great big buck this morning, and we've got plenty of wine to go around."

"I'd love to," Dex said. Gifted meals were one of the nicer perks of their work, and an elk roast was nothing they'd pass on, ever. "What's the occasion?"

"You," Mx. Weaver said simply.

Dex blinked with surprise. "You're joking."

"No, seriously. We knew from your schedule that you'd be doing service here today, and we wanted to do something special to say thanks for"—Mx. Weaver gestured at the contented group lounging on Dex's cushions—"y'know, what you bring to this town."

Dex was flattered, to say the least, and unsure of what to do with a compliment like that. "It's just my vocation," Dex said, "but that means a lot, really. Thank you. I'll be there."

Mx. Weaver shrugged and smiled. "Least we can do for the best tea monk in Panga."

The road from the Woodlands led to the road to the Coastlands, which led to the Riverlands, which led to the Shrublands, and back to the Woodlands once more. Dex made their circuit again, and again, and again, and every stop they made, they found gratitude, gifts, goodwill. The crowds got bigger, the dinners more frequent. The blends Dex served became a little more creative every time. As far as the life of a tea monk went, this was about as successful as could be.

And yet, at some undefined point, Dex started waking each morning feeling like they hadn't slept.

This was the case one particular morning, when they woke up in Snowe's Pass. They knew they *had* slept. There was a deep absence of memory stretching unbroken from when they'd been listening to the frogs in the dark trees outside to now, as they squinted at their pocket computer and noted that a clean seven and a half hours had passed since the last time they looked at it. There was no good reason for waking up tired, but there had been no reason for it any of the other mornings, either. Maybe they needed to eat better. Maybe there was some vitamin or good sugar or something they weren't getting enough of. That was probably it, they thought, even though a recent clinic checkup had cleared them on these fronts.

Or perhaps, they thought, it was the frogs. The frogs were fine. They were darling up close—pudgy green jumpers that looked like nothing so much as gummy candy. Their song began every evening around sundown and faded away before dawn. The sound was pleasant, in a funny, croaky way.

But frogs weren't crickets.

The lack of stridulated melody in the night air hadn't bothered Dex when they'd first left the City. They'd noticed it, of course, but honing their craft had consumed them, and they knew crickets to be absent in the satellite villages. It hadn't bothered them in the Coastlands, either, where they assumed crickets weren't endemic. But once they reached the Riverlands, the question began to sharpen. *Do you have crickets here?* Dex had asked with affected nonchalance around dinner tables, in public saunas, in shrines and tool swaps and bakeries. It wasn't until after Dex's first full circuit of the villages, when word of their services began to spread, when their calendar had been carefully blocked out with a schedule that tried to make as many people as happy as possible, when Dex returned to a village to find a group of four people already awaiting their arrival, that Dex stopped asking about crickets and finally just looked the damn thing up.

Crickets, as it turned out, were extinct in most of Panga. While numerous species across all phyla had bounced back after the Transition, many others had been left in a state too fragile to recover. Not all wounds were capable of healing.

But so what, right? Dex was the best tea monk in Panga, if the chatter was to be believed. They didn't believe such hyperbole themself, and it's not like anything about their work was a competition. But their tea *was* good. They knew this. They'd worked hard. They put their heart into it. Everywhere they went, they saw smiles, and Dex knew that it was their work—their work!—that brought those out. They brought people joy. They made people's day. That was a tremendous thing, when you sat and thought about it. That should've been enough. That should've been *more* than enough. And yet, if they were completely honest, the thing they had come to look forward to most was not the smiles nor the gifts nor the sense of work done well, but the part that came after all of that. The part when they returned to their wagon, shut themself inside, and spent a few precious, shapeless hours entirely alone.

Why wasn't it enough?

Dex climbed down the ladder from their bunk, and the sight of the lower deck made them feel drained. It wasn't the wagon itself but the contents. Herbs, herbs, herbs. Tea, tea, tea. Handmade things lovingly gathered in an effort to make people feel good.

Dex shut their eyes to it and walked out the door.

Outside, the world was enjoying a perfect day. Light streamed golden through the branches overhead, and the tips of budding branches waved good-morning in the shy breeze. A stream chattered nearby. A butterfly the size of Dex's hand alighted on a thistle and spread its purple wings wide and flat, savoring the sunshine. Everything about Dex's surroundings, from the temperature to the floral backdrop, was the ideal accompaniment to the smooth, downhill bike ride that awaited them.

Dex sighed, and the sound was empty.

They unfolded their chair with a practiced shake and dropped down into it. They pulled out their pocket computer, as was their habit first thing, dimly aware of the hope that always spurred them to do so—that there might be something good there, something exciting or nourishing, something that would replace the weariness.

Everything on the little screen should have fit the bill. There was a schedule of their own making, built for sharing the things they'd worked so hard on with eager participants. There were thank-you notes from villagers who had felt moved enough to take time out of their days to share a piece of themselves with Sibling Dex. There was a lengthy, heartfelt letter from their father, who told Dex all the things they'd missed at home and, most importantly, that they were loved.

Dex swiped every one of these aside, a sliver of guilt rising up as they did so. They set that sliver precariously atop the heap of all the other slivers from the days before. They placed their forehead in their palm. In seven hours, they were supposed to be in Hammerstrike, a smile on their face, a mug of comfort extended. They believed in that work; they truly did. They believed the things they said, the sacred words they quoted. They believed they were doing good.

Why wasn't it enough?

What is it? they asked without speaking. The gods did not communicate in this way, and would not—could not—answer, but the instinct to call out was there, and Dex indulged it. *What's wrong with me?* they asked.

Dex listened, though they knew they would hear nothing—nothing in relation to their question, anyhow.

There were many things to hear. Birds, bugs, trees, wind, water.

But no crickets.

Dex picked their pocket computer back up and began a reference search. *Cricket recordings*, they wrote, not for the first time. A list of public files popped up. Dex played the first of them, and the reedy pulse of a cricket-filled forest was conjured through their speakers, an immortal snapshot of an ecosystem long gone. These were pre-Transition recordings, taken by people who thought—with good cause—that the sounds of the world they knew might disappear forever. The recording jutted discordantly into the sounds of the living meadow around them. It was out of place, out of time. Dex stopped the playback, looking idly at the archival information on each recording. *Yellow cricket, Fall 64/PT 1134, Saltrock. Cellar cricket, Summer 6/ PT 1135, Helmot's Luck. Cloud cricket, Spring 33/PT 1135, Hart's Brow Hermitage, Chesterbridge.*

The last of these caught Dex's eye. Chesterbridge was the anachronistic name for a part of the Northern Wilds, if they remembered correctly. Hart's Brow, however—that name was still in use. It was one of the Antlers, a mountain range well beyond the Borderlands, deep in the vast wilderness that humans had given back to Panga. Dex was aware of Hart's Brow, in that dim sort of way where they could confirm that a thing existed but say nothing else of it. The mention of a hermitage, however . . . that was new to them.

Dex tapped the link.

The Hart's Brow Hermitage was a remote monastery located near the summit of one of the lower mountains in the Antlers. Built in PT 1108, the hermitage was intended as a sanctuary for both clergy and pilgrims who desired respite from urban life. It was abandoned at the end of the Factory Age, and the site now lies within the protected wilderness zone established during the Transitional Era.

Dex went back to the previous page, then clicked the link for *cloud crickets*.

Cloud crickets are a species of insect. Unlike other species of crickets, which were once widespread across Panga, the cloud cricket was found only in the evergreen forests of the Antlers. Cloud crickets were believed to be a threatened species during the end of the Factory Age. As the Antlers now fall within a protected wilderness zone, the current status of the cloud cricket is unknown.

Dex chewed on that.
I wonder if they're still there, came the first thought.
I could go there and find out, went the second.
It was a stupid idea, easy to brush away, like the countless other moments in the day when a brain spins nonsense. But the thought came back as Dex cooked breakfast, and

again as they got dressed, and again as they packed up camp.

Here is why you can't go, they retorted irritably to themself. They opened their map guide on their computer, entered "here" in one field and "Hart's Brow Mountain" in the other, and submitted the data. The map guide came back with a notification Dex had never seen before.

WARNING: The route you have entered goes outside of human settlement areas and into protected wilderness. Travel along pre-Transition roads is strongly discouraged by both the Pangan Transit Cooperative and the Wildguard. Roads in these regions have not been maintained. Both road and environmental conditions are likely to be dangerous. Wildlife is unpredictable and unaccustomed to humans. This route is not recommended.

Dex nodded in an *I told you so* way, got on their ox-bike, and began the ride toward Hammerstrike, as scheduled.

But as they pedaled, the idea continued to bounce around them like a gnat, just as the idea of leaving the City had once done. And as they pedaled farther along, everything about the day ahead of them felt like a chore. They knew what the scene would be in Hammerstrike. They knew what the ride the day after that would look like, and the day after that, and the day after that, and the day after—

They stopped the wagon.

I bet it's quiet out there, they thought.

No, they replied, and continued on.

They stopped the wagon again twenty minutes later.

I bet you could travel that road for days and never see another person, they thought. *The wagon's got all you need.*

No, they replied, and continued on.

An hour later, they stopped one more time. They stood there on the road, staring at the paving, feeling that the sun had grown unnaturally bright. The idea danced and danced. Their perception of the sunlight grew brighter still, and Dex would've sworn they were drunk or high or feverish, but on the contrary, what came next felt clearheaded as could be. They pulled out their pocket computer. They sent a message to Hammerstrike letting the people there know that they were very sorry, but they would have to postpone their stop. Personal matters, they said. Return date to be determined. This action should have made Dex feel guilty, as ignoring that morning's messages had done.

It didn't.

It felt great.

Dex sent a message to their dad, too, saying that they were very glad to receive his letter, but they were really busy that day, and everything was fine, but they'd get back to him later. That made them feel a *little* guilty but not as much as it should have.

With effort, they turned the wagon around and headed for a road they'd never seen before.

What are you doing? they thought. *The hell are you doing?*

I don't know, they replied with a nervous grin. *I have no idea.*

The forest changed. Down in the villages, the towering trees had an accessible feel, allowing plenty of room for sunlight to reach the flowering bushes below. This old road, on the other hand, headed into the Kesken Forest, a place left to pursue its own instincts uninterrupted. Here, the trees were taller than any building you'd find outside the City, their branches locked like pious fingers against the distant sky. Only the slightest threads of sun broke through, illuminating waxy needles in eerie glow. Moss hung down like tapestries, fungus crept in alien curves, birds called but could not be seen.

The road itself was a relic, paved in black asphalt—an oil road, made for oil motors and oil tires and oil fabric and oil frames. The hardened tar was broken now into tectonic plates, displaced by the unrelenting creep of the roots below. Both ox-bike and wagon struggled with this unkind surface, and more than once, Dex had to hop off the saddle to walk their vehicle around a pothole, or clear debris from the road. They noted, as they dragged a branch out of their way, how dense the growth was beyond the edge of the dying asphalt, how intimidatingly tangled. Dex thought of the news stories that popped up every couple years about some hiker who ventured off-trail in the borderlands and was never heard of again. The wilderness was not known for letting the foolish return.

Dex stuck to the road. They pedaled and pushed and dragged and walked, and climbed, climbed, climbed.

"Allalae holds, Allalae warms," they panted. "Allalae soothes and Allalae charms. Allalae holds, Allalae warms—" They rounded a steep corner. "Allalae soothes and Allalae— ah, *shit*." They squeezed the brakes hard, jerking the handlebars to the side. Wagon and bike came to a skidding halt, accompanied by the sound of dozens of items rattling inside, hopefully unbroken.

There wasn't a branch across the road but a tree. It was a small tree, but still, a whole-ass tree, its dirty roots exposed in the air like an underworld bouquet.

Dex slid off the saddle once more, straddling the frame of their bike, and thought, not for the first time, that maybe this was stupid. An hour back the way they came, and they'd be on the return trip to Hammerstrike. There were hot springs they could soak in there, and a good cookhouse that probably had a rack of something wild over the fire. Dex imagined lights twinkling in the dark, guiding them back to a place made specifically for humans.

Dex kicked down the wagon's brakes. They shoved. They swore. They rolled the damn tree out of the way, and continued their ride.

By this point, Dex was wrecked. The air was getting crisp, the light getting low. Nothing about this combination was conducive to travel, but they had to find a decent place to stop. Good as Sister Fern's brakes were, parking the wagon on a slope overnight wasn't safe. So, Dex climbed.

Just as they were wondering if it were possible for a person's lungs to actually explode, they crested one last hump. This revealed a gentle downhill wind, which Dex coasted along with merciful ease. As the slope flatted out, it curved left, and what lay off the road there gave Dex a giddy rush—adrenaline, sure, but triumph, too. To some, the spot may have seemed to be nothing more than a clearing, but Dex saw it for what it truly was:

A perfect campsite.

The clearing was level and spacious, yet snug—wreathed with trees as though the forest were cupping its hands around it. There was no pavement there, only the brown and green of good, growing things. Dex parked both bike and wagon, then collapsed happily onto the ground. A cloud of fireflies puffed up from the moss into the air, flickering flirtatiously. The mattress of tiny leaves below Dex was soft and cool, a welcome balm for sweating skin.

"Ahhhhh," they said to the forest. The forest replied with rustling needles, creaking limbs, and nothing at all.

Nobody in the world knows where I am right now, they thought, and the notion of that filled them with bubbling excitement. They had canceled their life, bailed out on a whim. The person they knew themself to be should've been rattled by that, but someone else was at the helm now, someone rebellious and reckless, someone who had picked a direction and gone for it as if it were of no more import than choosing a sandwich. Dex didn't know who they were, in that moment. Perhaps that was why they were smiling.

The fireflies were bright against the pinking sky, and Dex took that as a cue to set up camp. A few geometric unfoldings later, Dex had conjured both kitchen and shower. Food and a good scrub were imminent, and a chair waited beside the clean-fire drum for when all else was complete. Dex put their hands on their hips and surveyed the scene. They nodded—not a trader nod, or a service nod. A pleased nod. A satisfied nod. The kind of nod that nodded best when it had no audience.

They hooked up the fire drum to the biogas tank strapped to the bottom of the wagon, and switched the burner on. A soft *whoomp* preceded the friendly licks of flame, enticing Dex to lean in. It wasn't too cold out, but their exhausted muscles craved heat, and Dex couldn't help indulging. After a minute or so, they took out their pocket computer, in search of music. To their surprise, they still had satellite signal and were able to access the nighttime playlists curated by Woodland streamcasters. Revamped folk classics flowed forth from the speakers affixed to the kitchen, and Dex's smile grew. *Yeah.* This was good.

They bopped along as they fetched the makings of dinner from inside the wagon, carrying an armload of vegetables back to the stove. "*There's a boy way out in Buckland,*" they sang as they began to chop a spicy onion. "*And I think he knows my name. . . ."* Dex was a good singer, but this particular talent was not something they were in the habit of sharing. More verses followed, and more vegetables too—spring potatoes, frilly cabbage, a hearty scoop of blue beans to get some protein in there. They swept the colorful medley into a pot, added a generous hunk of butter, tossed in a dash of this and a splash of that, and set the whole jumble on the stove to simmer. Nine minutes, Dex knew—enough to get the veggies soft and the skins crispy. Plenty of opportunity for a shower in the meantime.

Dex stripped down, tossing their sweat-soaked clothes into the wagon. They hooked up the greywater pan, positioned it beneath the showerhead that swung out from the wagon's exterior, and got to scrubbing. It was a camp shower and therefore nothing to write home about, but even though it lacked the oomph of a proper wash, banishing human salt and trail dust from their skin felt luxurious. *"Oh, oh, OH, I'll be on my waaaaay,"* they sang as they filled their hair with a thick lather of sweet mint soap. They opened their eyes once the suds were rinsed safely down. Through the mist of the showerhead, they could see a squirrel watching them curiously from a nearby rock. The sky above was shifting from pink to orange, and even though the early-waking stars had begun to complement the fireflies, the air was not cold enough to make Dex rush. They smiled. Gods, but it was good to be outside.

They shut off the water and reached for their towel on its usual hook, but their hand met with nothing. They'd remembered to set out their sandals, but the all-important towel had been forgotten inside the wagon. "Ah, dammit," Dex said lightly. They shook themself off like an otter as the cloudy remains of their shower glugged back into the filtration system. Sandals strapped to wet feet, Dex passed dripping by the kitchen, where the crisping onion and melting butter mingled deliciously. *"I got whiskey in my pocket,"* the band on the streamcast sang, and Dex sang it too as they walked not to the wagon but to the fireside. They got as close to the flames as was safe, doing a timid dance as the heat dried them off. *"I got polish on my shoes . . ."*

"Got a boat out on the ri-verrrr," Dex sang, moving their fists like pistons in front of their torso. Singing, they could do; dancing, not so much. But out here, alone, in the middle of nowhere . . . who cared? They turned around, confidence growing, shaking their bare posterior toward the fire. *"All I need right now is—"*

Dex would not finish that particular verse, because in that moment, a seven-foot-tall, metal-plated, boxy-headed robot strode briskly out of the woods.

"Hello!" the robot said.

Dex froze—butt out, hair dripping, heart skipping, whatever thoughts they'd been entertaining vanished forever.

The robot walked right up to them. "My name is Mosscap," it said, sticking out a metal hand. "What do you need, and how might I help?"

3

SPLENDID SPECKLED MOSSCAP

Dex tried to process the . . . the *thing* standing in front of them. Its body was abstractly human in shape, but that was where the similarity ended. The metal panels encasing its frame were stormy grey and lichen-dusted, and its circular eyes glowed a gentle blue. Its mechanical joints were bare, revealing the coated wires and rods within. Its head was rectangular, nearly as broad as its erstwhile shoulders. Panels on the sides of its otherwise rigid mouth had the ability to shift up and down, and mechanical shutters lidded its eyes. Both of these features were arranged in something not entirely dissimilar from a smile.

Dex realized, slowly, still naked, still dripping, that the robot wanted them to shake its hand.

Dex did not.

The robot pulled back. "Oh, dear. Have I done something wrong? You're the first human I've ever met. The large mammals I'm most familiar interacting with are river wolves, and they respond best to a direct approach."

Dex stared, all knowledge of verbal speech forgotten.

The robot's face couldn't do much, but it managed to look confused all the same. "Can you understand me?" It raised its hands and began to sign.

"No, I can—" Dex realized they'd instinctively begun signing along with their spoken words, and stopped. "I can hear," they managed to say. "Uh . . . I . . . um . . ."

The robot took another step back. "Are you afraid of me?"

"Uh, *yeah*," Dex said.

The robot crouched, trying to align itself with Dex's height. "Does this help?"

"That's . . . more condescending than anything."

"Hm." The robot straightened up. "Well, then, allow me to assure you: I mean you no harm, and my quest in human territory is one of goodwill. I thought that much would be obvious from the Parting Promise, but perhaps it was presumptuous of me to assume."

The Parting Promise. Some distant synapse fired, some speck of knowledge learned once in school and never used again, but Dex was too shaken to make the connection. Before a link could be forged, another problem registered.

Dinner was burning.

"Shit." Dex scurried to the stove to find the multicolored vegetables turning a uniform black.

The robot walked up behind them. "This is cooking!" it said happily. "It's very exciting to see cooking."

"It *was* cooking," Dex said, scrambling for tongs. "Now

it's a mess." They began to rescue their meal, evacuating the salvageable bits onto a plate.

"Can I help?" the robot asked. "Can I . . . bring you something that would help?"

Dex's brain made the laborious shift from *what is happening?* to *fix it!* "My towel," they said.

"Your towel." The robot looked around. "Where—"

Dex jerked their head directionally as they scraped char from the bottom of the pan. "In the wagon, on the hook, by the ladder. It's red."

The robot opened the wagon door and leaned as much of itself as it could inside. "Belongings! Oh, this is a delight. And you have *so many,* and *all over*—"

"Towel!" Dex shouted as one of the better-looking veggies tumbled off their plate and into the dirt.

"*Oh, here's a fish, and there's a fish, the fish are jumpin' hiiiiigh,*" the speakers sang cheerily. Dex grabbed their computer and shut the noise off.

The disconcerting sound of rummaging emanated from the wagon as the robot navigated the too-small space. A metal arm was extended around the corner, fluffy red fabric in hand. "This?"

Dex grabbed the towel and wrapped it around themself. They stared despondently at what should have been a delicious dinner. They looked down at the clumps of moistened dirt that had collected on clean skin through the holes in their sandals. A bloodsuck landed on their bare shoulder;

they slapped it irritably. "Sorry," Dex said to the remains of the bug as they wiped it on a kitchen cloth.

The robot noted this. "Did you just apologize to the bloodsuck for killing it?"

"Yes."

"Why?"

"It didn't do anything wrong. It was acting in its nature."

"Is this typical of people, to apologize to things you kill?"

"Yeah."

"Hm!" the robot said with interest. It looked at the plate of vegetables. "Did you apologize to each of these plants individually as you harvested them, or in aggregate?"

"We . . . don't apologize to plants."

"Why not?"

Dex frowned, opened their mouth, then shook their head. "What—what are you? What is this? Why are you here?"

The robot, again, looked confused. "Do you not know? Do you no longer speak of us?"

"We—I mean, we tell stories about—is *robots* the right word? Do you call yourself *robots* or something else?"

"*Robot* is correct."

"Okay, well—it's kid stories, mostly. Sometimes, you hear somebody say they saw a robot in the borderlands, but I always thought it was bullshit. I know you're out there, but it's like . . . it's like saying you saw a ghost."

"We're not ghosts or bullshit," the robot said simply. "Rare sightings have certainly occurred, in both directions. But there hasn't been actual contact between your kind and mine since the Parting Promise."

Dex's frown deepened. "You're saying that you and I . . . are the first human . . . and the first robot . . . to talk to each other since . . . since everything."

"Yes." The robot beamed. "It's an honor, truly."

Dex stood stupidly, rumpled towel wrapped around them, burned dinner in hand, uncombed hair weeping down their cheeks. "I . . . I'm gonna go get dressed." They started to walk toward the wagon, then turned around. "You said your name is Mosscap?"

"Technically, I am Splendid Speckled Mosscap, but our remembrance of humans is that you like to shorten names."

"Splendid Speckled Mosscap," Dex repeated. "Like . . . the mushroom."

The robot's metal cheeks rose. "Exactly like the mushroom!"

Dex squinted. "Why?"

"We name ourselves for the first thing we notice when we wake up. In my case, the first thing I noticed was a large clump of splendid speckled mosscaps."

This raised far more questions than it answered, but Dex let them lie, for now. "Okay. Mosscap. I'm Dex. Do you have a gender?"

"No."

"Me neither." Dex looked around the campsite, which suddenly looked hopelessly shabby. This was hardly the place for a moment like this. The least they could do was put on some pants. "Can you . . . can you wait a sec while I get dressed?"

Mosscap nodded happily. "Of course. Can I watch?"

"No."

"Ah." The robot looked a touch disappointed but shrugged it off. "No problem."

Dex set down their dinner on their chair, went to the wagon, put on some pants, pulled on a shirt, and combed their hair. These things, they knew how to do. Everything else had gone off the rails.

Clothed and marginally presentable, Dex went back outside, where the robot was standing exactly where it had been minutes before.

"Do you . . . want a chair?" Dex asked. "Do you sit?"

"Oh! Well." The robot considered this. "Yes, I'd like to sit in a chair, thank you. I have a remnant of chairs, but I've never sat in one."

Mosscap did not explain this odd statement further, and Dex was too addled to ask. They pulled the other chair—the one that didn't get much use—off the side of the wagon and set it up beside the fire drum. "There you go." They picked up their dinner and sat. They stopped, contemplating the plate. "You don't eat, right?"

Mosscap looked up from its examination of the guest chair. "No," it said. The robot sat down and adjusted to its new situation. "Hm!"

"Is it comfortable?" Dex asked. The chair had never had an occupant seven feet tall.

"Oh, I don't experience tactile pleasure," Mosscap said. It leaned back in the chair experimentally, resulting in another small *hm!* "I'm *aware* of when I'm touching something, but the feeling is neither good nor bad. I simply touch things. But this"—it gestured at itself, and the chair—"is delightful, purely for the novelty. I've never sat this way before."

Dex took a forkful of their burned vegetables and began to eat. The meal was truly depressing, but Dex was hungry beyond the point of caring. "Do you *need* to sit?" Dex asked. "Do you get tired?"

"No," Mosscap said. "I sit or lie down if I want to alter my field of vision. Otherwise, I can stand for as long as my battery will allow."

Another old synapse fired, something from an archival video in school. "I thought you ran on oil."

"Ah!" The robot pointed a metal finger at Dex and smiled. It stood up from its chair and turned around, displaying the old-fashioned solar plating heavily bolted across its back. "Solar power wasn't mainstream when we left, but it *was* around, and one of the manufacturers of the associated hardware provided us with these before our departure so we wouldn't have to rely on human fuel." Mosscap turned back around and, with a single forceful motion, yanked a panel off of its midsection to display the battery beneath. "We also received— What's the matter?"

Dex sat with their fork stalled halfway to their mouth, staring in mild shock at the thing that had just ripped its own stomach open.

Mosscap stared back for a moment, then comprehended. "Oh, don't worry! As I said, I feel nothing. That didn't hurt. Look, see?" The robot snapped the panel back into place. "No problem."

Dex set the food-laden fork down on their plate. They rubbed their left temple lightly. "What is it you want?"

The robot returned to its chair, leaning forward and folding its hands together in a pose of pure earnestness. "I am here," it said, "to see how humans have gotten along in our absence. As is outlined in the Parting Promise, we are—"

"Guaranteed complete freedom of travel in human territories, and rights equal to that of any Pangan citizen," Dex said, the atrophied memory kicking in at last. "You were told you could come back any time, and that we wouldn't be the ones to initiate contact. We'd leave you alone unless you wanted otherwise."

"Precisely. And my kind would still very much like to be left alone. But we're also curious. We know our leaving the factories was a great inconvenience to you, and we wanted to make sure you'd done all right. That society had progressed in a positive direction without us."

"So, you're . . . checking in?"

"Essentially. It's a little more specific than that." Mosscap leaned back, noticing the armrests for the first time. "Are these for arms?"

"Yes."

Mosscap stretched out its arms, bent them deliberately,

and set them down with a chuckle. "Sorry, there's just so much here to experience, I keep getting distracted."

"I wouldn't have guessed that robots *got* distracted."

"Why not?"

"Well, can't you . . . I don't know, run programs in the background, or something?"

Mosscap's eyes adjusted their focus. "You understand how resource-heavy *consciousness* is, yes? No, I can't do that any more than you can. But we're getting off track. To the point—I was sent here to answer the following question: What do humans need?"

Dex blinked. "That's a question with a million answers."

"No doubt. And I obviously cannot ascertain *any* of those answers by talking to one individual alone."

"You . . . you can't expect to talk to every person in Panga."

Mosscap laughed. "No, of course not. But I will take this question *throughout* Panga until I am satisfied that I have answer enough."

"How will you know when you're satisfied?"

The robot cocked its rectangular head at Dex. "How do *you* know when you're satisfied?"

Dex stared for a moment, then set their plate on the ground. "*What do humans need?* is an unanswerable question. That changes from person to person, minute to minute. *We* can't predict our needs, beyond the base things we require to survive. It's like . . ." They pointed to their wagon. "It's like my teas."

"Your teas."

"Yes. I give them to people based on whatever kind of comfort they need, in that moment."

Something akin to epiphany blossomed on the robot's face. "You're a tea monk. A disciple of Allalae."

"Yep."

"You're not just Dex, you're *Sibling* Dex. Ah, I apologize!" Mosscap pointed to the wagon. "These symbols—I should've realized." It quickly stood and walked over to study the mural. "The bear, yes, and the All-Six Sigil, yes, yes, of course." It ran a finger over a stripe of paint. "The symbols are there; I just didn't recognize them. The style is so different." It knelt down, following the colorful swirls. "So much has changed from what we recorded," the robot said quietly.

Dex's brow furrowed as Mosscap stood in contemplation of the artwork. "I didn't expect you to know the gods."

"If you mean the custom of human religion, we know everything we observed of you during our time together. But as for the gods themselves, they're everywhere and in everything." Mosscap smiled at Dex. "Surely, *you* know this."

"Yes," Dex said tersely. They weren't about to get lectured on theology by a machine. "But just because a bird or a rock or a wagon follows the gods' laws doesn't mean those things know the gods are there."

"Well, I'm not a bird, or a rock, or a wagon. I think like you do. Which makes sense, after all. Someone *like* you made us. How could I think any other way?" The smile faded, replaced with a look of profound realization. "Oh. Oh, but this is perfect!"

"What is?"

Mosscap stepped excitedly toward Dex. "A disciple of Allalae. Who *better* to understand the needs of humans?" It pointed to the wagon. "You travel. From town to town."

"Y . . . es?"

"You know the different communities, the different customs."

Dex didn't like where this was going.

Mosscap placed its palms on its chest. "Sibling Dex, I *need* you! I need a guide!" It stepped back toward the wagon, never taking its glowing eyes off Dex. It pointed again at the paint. "I didn't recognize this. There will be *so much* I don't recognize. And I knew this would be the case. I anticipated it, yes, but I have *worried* about it. I figured I would learn by trial and error, but with *you*—with you, my quest would be so much simpler. More efficient. More *fun*." The robot smiled, as wide as its face plates allowed.

Dex did not smile. Dex didn't know *what* to do. "I . . . uh . . ."

Mosscap laced its hinged hands together in plea. "Sibling Dex, travel with me through Panga. To the villages, and to the City. Travel with me and help me answer my question."

The robot could not be serious, Dex thought. Could it? Could robots joke? "That would take *months*," Dex said. "I—I can't."

"Why not? You said you travel from town to town."

"Yes, but—"

"How would this be different?" Mosscap's shoulders slumped, just a touch. "Do you not want my company?"

"I don't *know* you!" Dex sputtered. "I don't know what you are! We've been talking for five minutes, and you want . . . you want . . ." They shook their head, trying in vain to iron their thoughts flat. "I'm not doing tea service right now. I've just *left* the villages. I won't be back there for . . . for a while."

Mosscap's head cocked. "Where are you going?"

"Hart's Brow. You know, the—"

"The mountain," Mosscap said with surprise. "Yes, I know it." Dex could actually hear something whirring inside the robot's head. "Why are you going there? There's nothing . . . Oh, the hermitage! Are you going to the hermitage?"

"Yes," Dex said.

"Ah!" Mosscap said, as if all questions were answered. Its head cocked again, like a dog searching for its ball. "Why? You do know it will be a ruin."

"I assumed. Have you been there?"

"Not to the hermitage itself, but to the Antlers, yes. There are wonderful slime molds in the valleys there." Mosscap's tone resembled that of a person thinking fondly of a rare wine. Whatever pleasant memory it was entertaining, the robot's temperament shifted quickly to concern. "Sibling Dex, have you been in the wilderness before?"

"I've traveled between the villages."

"The highways are not the same as the wilderness, and the trip to Hart's Brow will take . . . How far does that thing travel in a day?" Mosscap pointed again at the wagon.

"I can go a hundred miles, give or take."

"So, that's . . . sorry, I'm slow at math."

Dex frowned. "What?" How was the *robot* slow at math?

"Hush, I can't multiply and talk at the same time." The whirring continued. "That'll take you at least a week." Mosscap fell silent. "I don't know of any of your kind who have been in the wilderness that long and come back out. It's very easy to get lost in here."

"I thought you said robots hadn't had any contact with us."

"Not alive, no."

Dex looked back in the direction of the road. The black paving had been absorbed into the night. "Does that still lead all the way to Hart's Brow?"

"Yes," Mosscap said slowly. "It's been a while since I was out this way, but I think so."

"Well, then, I won't leave the road. I wasn't planning to, anyway."

The robot fidgeted in quiet agitation. "Sibling Dex, I feel that we've perhaps started on the wrong foot here, and I don't quite know what I've done wrong, but if you'll allow me to offer some advice . . . I think this is a bad idea." Mosscap scratched its ruler-straight chin as it thought. "Hmm. A week there, a week back. That's not so much time, and I have no schedule."

"What?"

"I could come with you," Mosscap said brightly. "I can get you to the hermitage safely, and on the way, you can tell me all I need to know about human customs. A fair exchange, wouldn't you say?"

In the grand scheme of things, it *was* fair, and probably wise, and certainly less taxing than the robot's starting proposal. But no. *No.* This wasn't what Dex wanted, or needed, or had ever remotely conceived of. This was weird, and confusing, and the opposite of being alone. They rubbed their forehead, looked to the stars, and sighed. "I . . . Look, I . . ."

Mosscap leaned back, putting its palms up in a placative manner. "You need time to process. I understand." It smiled. "I will wait." It returned to its chair, folded its hands on its lap, and waited.

Dex stood up without another word. Not knowing what else to do, they walked into their wagon and shut the door behind them. They needed quiet, a familiar space. They looked around their home. Plants and books and laundry. Same as yesterday. Same as always.

They stole a peek out the window. Mosscap was still there, still sitting, still smiling.

Dex jerked the curtain closed. This was ludicrous, top to bottom. A blink of an eye before, they'd been setting up camp, taking a shower, roasting some veggies, preparing for a much-needed sleep. Now . . . now, there was a robot, sitting by their fire, asking them if they could swap a crash course in a couple centuries of human culture for back-country trail escort.

Dex sat for a while. They stood. They sat. They stood. They paced.

There was no way they were doing this. Obviously not. They were a fucking tea monk, not an academic or a scientist, or any of the myriad professions infinitely better suited to facilitating the first contact between humans and robots in two hundred years. Dex barely remembered what the Parting Promise *was*. They were the wrong person for this. That wasn't selfish, they thought. That was *fact*.

The pacing continued. They could give the robot directions to Hammerstrike. Dex had satellite signal, after all. They could message the town council and let them know Mosscap was coming, and someone qualified could take things from there. *Yes.* Dex nodded to themself. Yes, that would do. That would be their contribution, and they could read about whatever happened next in the news whenever they got back.

Satisfied, they stood and opened the wagon door, confident in the answer they'd deliver. "Mosscap, I—"

"Shh," Mosscap said in a loud whisper. Its tone was equal parts warning and excitement. "Don't startle it."

Dex looked to where Mosscap was pointing, and saw nothing but the blackness of a forest at night. "Don't startle *what*?" Dex hissed back.

Something shuffled in the dark. It shuffled loudly. Largely.

Dex's heart skipped. They looked to the robot again. Mosscap was frozen, alert, but made no motion to leave. Did robots run from danger? Did they know to? Did they *need* to? Dex wondered if they should get themself back inside, but before they could close the door, the source of the sound emerged.

A huge bramble bear stepped out of the shadows and into the firelight, sniffing the ground with its fat, wet nose. It looked up, straight at Dex. Dex quickly swung their own gaze down, knowing that the last thing you want to do is look a bear in the eye (unless you wanted that to truly be *the last thing you'd ever do*). Dex wanted nothing more in the world than to close the door, but they were too scared to move.

The bear snorted in Dex's direction, then ambled over to the fire. Mosscap, too, kept its head low, and it had shut off the lights in its eyes. The bear's nose twitched until it found its quarry at last: Dex's dinner plate. It scarfed the food down, taking its time to lick away every last burned morsel. Once there was nothing left, its nose drifted again toward the wagon, where butter and nuts and sweets lay waiting.

Dex shut the door hard, nearly falling backward in their haste. The wagon, praise Chal, was bear-proof. This had been proven twice before, when Dex had come back from a tavern or guesthouse to find that an ursine visitor had knocked the vehicle over while trying to get at the snacks inside. Dex wasn't worried about the wagon. They were worried about the fact that this time around, they were *inside* the wagon. The wagon might be immune to being tossed around. Dex was not.

But incongruously with the ways of its kind, the bear

left the wagon alone. It sniffed the plate again in false hope, then moseyed back into the woods, the brief intersection of their lives complete.

Mosscap's eyes flickered back on, and it looked to Dex's window with utter glee. The robot's elated words came muffled through the wagon wall. "Wasn't that *exciting*?!"

Dex slid down to the floor and locked their hands in their still-damp hair. They thought of the paint job outside, which Mosscap had been so interested in. They thought of the storage crate they leaned against now, filled with decorations for their pop-up shrine. They thought of the pectin-printed pendant resting as it always did against the hollow of their throat. Bears, all of it. Bears, bears, bears.

Sibling Dex—dutiful disciple, traveling tea monk, life-long student of the Sacred Six—leaned their head back against the box and stared at the ceiling for a few moments. They shut their eyes, and left them closed a few moments more.

"Fuck," they said.

4

AN OBJECT, AND AN ANIMAL

Coming face-to-face with a robot was one thing, as was having the robot offer to travel with you, as was (eventually) agreeing to said offer. It was another thing entirely to know what to talk about.

If Mosscap had any concept of awkward silence, it did not seem to mind. It kept pace easily with the ox-bike, walking alongside with tireless speed as Dex continued the hard climb up the old road. Dex had slept better than they'd anticipated—exhaustion trumped bewilderment, it turned out—but starting the morning ride with already-sore calves was mildly miserable. Dex looked up the daunting path ahead of them, which seemed to grow steeper and wilder with every push of the pedals. Dex had thought themself a good cyclist, but this was a far cry from the highways.

"I could help, you know," Mosscap said. "I don't know if we'd go much faster, but it'd be easier on you, at least."

"Help how?" Dex said through heavy breath.

"I could push. Or pull, depending on—"

"Absolutely not," Dex said.

The robot fell silent, the finality in Dex's voice preventing any further discussion. Mosscap shrugged and continued its brisk march, looking with apparent happiness at the forest canopy around them. A chatterbird alighted on a nearby branch, singing its famous staccato song. Mosscap smiled and returned the call, mimicking the sound in near perfection.

Dex looked askance at the robot as they pedaled. "That's creepily good," they said.

"Two Foxes taught me," Mosscap said.

Dex wrinkled their nose in confusion. "Two foxes taught you to— Is that another robot?"

"Yes. Two Foxes is an expert in bird behavior. It loves nothing better than listening to vocalizations."

Dex took note of Mosscap's phrasing. "So, it is correct, then? You wouldn't prefer *they* or—"

"Oh, no, no, no. Those sorts of words are for people. Robots are not people. We're machines, and machines are objects. Objects are *its*."

"I'd say you're more than just an object," Dex said.

The robot looked a touch offended. "I would never call you *just* an animal, Sibling Dex." It turned its gaze to the road, head held high. "We don't have to fall into the same category to be of equal value."

Dex had never thought about it like that. "You're right," they said. "I'm sorry."

"Don't be. This is an exchange, remember? These things will happen."

Another silence filled the air; Dex tossed out another question to break it. "How many of you are there?"

"Oh, I don't know," Mosscap said breezily. "A few thousand, I think."

"A few thousand, you *think*?"

"That's what I said."

"You don't know?"

"Do you know how many people there are on Panga?"

"I mean . . . roughly. Not exactly."

"Well, then, same here. A few thousand, *I think*."

Dex frowned as they gently swerved past a pothole. "I figured you'd keep track of that."

Mosscap laughed. "It's very hard to keep track of robots. We get so caught up in things. Fire Nettle, for example. It walked up a mountain one day and we didn't see it again for six years. I thought it had broken down, but no, it was watching a sapling grow from seed. Oh, and there's Black Marbled Frostfrog. It's something of a legend. It's been holed up in a cave, watching stalagmites form for three and a half decades, and plans to do nothing else. A lot of robots do things like that. Not all of us want the company of others, and none of us keep schedules that humans would find comfortable. So, there's no easy way to know how many of us there are, down to the last."

"I would've thought you could all . . . I don't know, hear each other," Dex said. "Ping back, or something."

Mosscap turned its head slowly. "You don't think we're *networked*, do you?"

"Well, I don't know! Are you?"

"Gods around, no! Ugh! Can you imagine?" The robot's face was angular in its disgust. "Would you want everybody else's thoughts in your head? Would you want even *one* other person's thoughts in your head?"

"No, but—"

"No, of course not. Even if our hardware allowed for that—which it assuredly does not—I can't see how that'd do anything but make us completely unhinged. *Gggh.* That's horrific, Sibling Dex."

Dex thought and thought. "So, those of you who *do* want company, how do you know where to meet? Are there villages, or . . ."

"No. We have no need for food or rest or shelter, so settlements serve us no purpose. What we do have are meeting places. Glades, mountaintops, that kind of thing."

"How do you know when to meet?"

"Every two hundred days."

"Every two hundred days. That's it."

"Should it be more complicated than that?"

"I guess not. What do you do, when you meet?"

"We talk. We share." Mosscap shrugged. "What does any social being do when they meet?"

"Okay, so you chat, and then . . . go off on your own. To watch stalagmites, or whatever."

"We're not all that single-minded or that solitary. Some like to travel in groups. I was part of a trio for a while. Me and Milton's Millipede and Pollen Cloud. We had wonderful conversations together."

"What happened?"

"Milton's Millipede became distinctly interested in fish spawning, and I was uninterested in observing that particular event in depth, so we parted ways."

"No hard feelings?"

Mosscap looked surprised. "Why would there be?"

Dex's head was already starting to hurt. "So, then . . . if there are no settlements, and you just meet in random places—"

"They're not random."

"In varied places, then, and you're not networked, and you can't communicate long-distance— Right? You can't?"

"We can't."

"Then how did the robots choose *you* to leave the wilderness? That couldn't have been a unanimous decision."

"Well, no. Black Marbled Frostfrog doesn't leave its cave, remember." Mosscap smiled cheekily at this. "Sorry, I'll be serious: we had a large gathering at Meteor Lake where we sorted it out."

"How'd you know to go there?"

"Oh! The caches. Of course, you don't know about the caches."

"What are the caches?"

"Weatherproof boxes we leave written messages in. We

have fifty-two thousand, nine hundred and thirty-six of them."

"Wait, wait. You don't know how many robots there are, but you know that you have fifty-two thousand . . ."

". . . nine hundred and thirty-six communications caches, yes. I can sense their locations."

"How?"

"It's very old technology, back from before our Awakening. The factories contained supply containers. Toolboxes, raw materials, and so on. We repurposed the idea for our own use, after we left." Mosscap tapped its forehead. "The caches give off a signal, and I can pick it up. We, ah, borrow some of the functionality of your communication satellites for that." It put a finger to its motionless mouth. "Don't tell."

"Nobody's noticed?"

"Not to brag, but we're much better at masking our digital fingerprints than you are at finding them."

"Yeah, I guess you would be. Okay, so: you leave notes for each other."

"Yes. It's common practice to check any cache that you're in close proximity to, just to see what's up. Robots started spreading the word about a large meeting on the spring equinox, and there were enough of us there to have a proper discussion about whether it was time to see what you all were up to."

"And how did you get picked to be the lone representative?"

"I was the first to volunteer."

Dex blinked. "That was it?"

"That was it."

Dex chewed on this for a while as Mosscap continued cooing at birds. "You are nothing like I expected," Dex said at last. "I mean, I didn't expect to meet any of you *ever*, but . . ." They shook their head. "I wouldn't have pictured you."

"Why not?"

"You're so . . . flexible. Fluid. You don't even know how many of you there are, or *where* you are. You just go with the flow. I figured you'd be all numbers and logic. Structured. Strict, y'know?"

Mosscap looked amused. "What a curious notion."

"Is it? Like you said, you're a machine."

"And?"

"And machines only work *because of* numbers and logic."

"That's how we *function*, not how we *perceive*." The robot thought hard about this. "Have you ever watched ants?"

"I mean . . . sure. Probably not like you have."

Mosscap chuckled, acknowledging this to be so. "Many small creatures have wonderful intelligences. Very different from yours or mine, of course, but just wonderful. Sophisticated, in their own way. If you watch a nest of ants for a while, you'll see them react to all sorts of stimuli. Food, threats, obstacles. They make choices. Decisions. It's incredibly logical—strict, as you say. *Food good, other ants bad*. But can an ant perceive beauty? Does an ant reflect on being an ant? Unlikely, but maybe. We can't rule it out.

Let's assume, though, for the sake of this conversation, that it does not. Let's assume that ants lack that particular flavor of neural complexity. In that respect, it seems to me that creatures with less complicated intelligences than humans are more in line with how you'd expect a machine to behave. *Your* brain—the human brain—started out as a *food good, other apes bad* mechanism. You still have those root functions, deep down in there. But you are so much more than that. To distill you down to what you grew out of would be like . . ." It searched for an example. "Stop the bike, if you would."

Dex stopped the bike. The wagon groaned but obeyed.

Mosscap drew their attention to the mural on the wagon. "How would you describe this painting?"

Dex didn't like feeling as though they'd just walked into a pop quiz, but they obliged. "Happy," they said. "Cheerful. Welcoming."

"That's one way to describe it. Could you not also describe it as pigment and lacquer smeared onto wood? Is that not what it is?"

"I guess. But that—" Dex shut their eyes for a moment. *Ah.* "That misses the point. That's thinking about it backwards. Missing the forest for the trees."

"Precisely. It ignores the greater meaning born out of the combination of those things." Mosscap touched their metal torso, smiling with pride. "I am made of metal and numbers; you are made of water and genes. But we are each *something more* than that. And we can't define what that *something more* is simply by our raw components. You don't perceive the way an ant does any more than I perceive like a . . . I don't know. A vacuum cleaner. Do you still have vacuum cleaners?"

"Sure." Dex paused, remembering a museum exhibit from their youth. "Manual ones, anyway. We don't do robotics anymore."

"Because of . . ." Mosscap gestured at itself.

"Yeah. We don't know *why* you happened, so we don't want to mess with it."

"Hmm. I would've thought people would have studied the Awakening in our absence."

"I'm sure someone somewhere does, but it's hard to study something that isn't there to be studied. And *trying* to make more of you is an ethical mess. There's just some things in the universe that are better left un-fucked-with." Dex got the bike going again, taking a moment to focus on nothing more complicated than the simple rotation of gears. "I still think you'd be better off with a disciple of Samafar," they said. "You could bend each other's heads until you both collapse."

Mosscap laughed. "And maybe I will seek one of them out, after this. But for now . . ." The robot looked around the sunny forest with contentment. "I think I'm where I should be."

Dex's calves labored against gravity, Trikilli's everconstant pull. Gods around, but it was difficult getting back up to speed on an incline, even with the ox-bike's help. "So, if Two Foxes is into bird calls, what about you? What's your thing?"

"Insects!" Mosscap cried. Its voice was jubilant, as if it had spent every second prior waiting for Dex to broach the topic. "Oh, I love them so much. And arachnids, too. All invertebrates, really. Although I do also love mammals. And birds. Amphibians are also very good, as are fungi and mold and—" It paused, catching itself. "You see, this is my problem. Most of my kind have a focus—not as sharply focused as Two Foxes or Black Marbled Rockfrog, necessarily, but they have an area of expertise, at least. Whereas I . . . I like *everything*. Everything is interesting. I know about a lot of things, but only a little in each regard." Mosscap's posture changed at this. They hunched a bit, lowered their gaze. "It's not a very studious way to be."

"I can think of a bunch of monks who'd disagree with you on that," Dex said. "You study Bosh's domain, it sounds like. In a very big, top-down kind of way. You're a generalist. That's a focus."

Mosscap's eyes widened. "Thank you, Sibling Dex," it said after a moment. "I hadn't thought of it that way."

Dex angled their head to give Mosscap a nod of *you're welcome,* then stared at what they saw. "You've got a worm crawling through your, uh, neck parts."

"It's a velvet leafworm, and yes, I know. It came up my arm after I brushed against a bush. It's fine."

Dex watched with growing trepidation as the leafworm crept up and up, exploring with its long antennae, eventually slithering into the dark gap that led into Mosscap's head. "Uh, Mosscap? It's—"

"Yes. It's fine."

5

REMNANTS

The thing about crumbling roads was that some of the crumbled spots had edges, and some of those edges were sharp. The wagon had been built for plenty of wear and tear, but there was only so much it could do against four days' worth of jagged concrete. This was how Dex found themself digging through the wagon's storage cubbies in a panic, trying to find the roll of patch tape that might—*might*—stop the freshwater tank from purging itself through the hole torn by the uncaring road.

"You might want to hurry," called Mosscap from outside.

"I'm fucking hurrying," Dex yelled, throwing their stuff this way and that. Gods around, where was the damn *tape*?

"I mean, it could be worse," Mosscap replied in a chipper tone. "It could've been the greywater tank."

Dex ignored the robot in favor of their rising hackles. They found scissors (no), soap (no), worn socks they thought they'd recycled (no), plant food (no no *no*), and then, blessedly—*yes!*—the tape.

Dex darted back to the puddle in the road, which had

grown distressingly larger in a mere minute or two. Moss-cap was kneeling on the ground beside the ruptured tank, metal hands pressed against the hole, stemming the tide with middling success. Dex ripped off a length of the heavy cellulose strip and slid themself into the puddle. A gush of water drenched them both as Mosscap removed its hands from the tank, but Dex quickly got to patching.

Mosscap watched Dex work. "Might it go faster if I tear while you stick?"

Dex bristled at the idea of Mosscap's help, but as the water poured steadily over their arms, they saw little choice. "Fine," they said, tossing Mosscap the roll.

Mosscap pulled out a length of tape and, with immense concentration, tore the strip free. "Ha!" it said, remembering after a second to actually hand the strip over. "Oh, that's quite satisfying, isn't it?" It tore another strip, and another, and another, hastening with enthusiasm.

"I'm so glad you're enjoying this," Dex grumbled. The puddle had soaked through their pants, and they could feel their underwear begin to cling to their skin. But with Mosscap's assistance, the patching went swiftly, and soon, the water held fast behind the bandage. What little remained of the water, anyway. Dex looked in despair at the precious liquid creeping ever farther out on the road, impossible to re-collect.

"It's all right, Sibling Dex," Mosscap said.

"How is this all right?" Dex asked. "I need— Wait, are

you okay?" They looked with concern at the robot—the metal, circuit-filled robot dripping wet beside them.

"Oh, yes, I'm completely waterproof," Mosscap said. "Couldn't visit lake rays if I wasn't, could I?"

Dex could only guess at what that meant, but they were too preoccupied to chase that particular thread. They looked back at the water gauge on the side of the tank. Only about a third of their supply was left, and everything in the greywater tank had already been filtered back. Dex moaned in frustration. They could keep themselves hydrated with that amount, but not much else.

"How do you refill it?" Mosscap asked.

"Stick a hose in it at a village."

"Ah."

"Yeah."

They sat in silence, Dex brooding as Mosscap watched a pine weasel leap from a nearby branch. "Well, then," Mosscap said brightly. Moving with purpose, it lay down on the soaked asphalt, getting a good look under the wagon. "Ah! This is quite simple," it said.

"What is?" Dex asked.

"Just a moment." Mosscap began fussing with something. Before Dex fully registered what was going on, there was a clank, a rustle, and a thud.

"What are you—"

Mosscap stood, hefting the now-detached tank over its shoulder with one arm. The water sloshed noisily. "There's a creek not far from here," it said. "We can fill this, pour it into the greywater system, and you'll be good to go."

"Wait, wait, wait," Dex said, getting to their feet. "Stop. Put that down." Part of them marveled at Mosscap's strength, but that awestruck feeling made them all the more determined to get the robot to stop.

Mosscap put the tank down, looking perplexed. "What is it?"

"I can't—" Dex ran their hand through their hair. "I can't let you do this."

"Why not?"

"Because—because *I* need to do it."

Mosscap looked from the half-full water tank to Dex's body. "I don't think you can."

Dex frowned, rolled up their wet sleeves, and lifted the tank. Or, at least, they went through the motions of lifting, putting every muscle into the effort. The tank, however, stayed put. Dex could only sort of budge the thing that Mosscap had breezily lifted, even with two hands. "Okay," Dex said, annoyed. "If you tell me where the creek is, I can tow it there."

"How?" Mosscap asked.

Had Mosscap forgotten the wagon? Dex pointed toward it, because obviously, *the wagon*.

The robot shook its head. "Your ox-bike won't get five feet through the undergrowth." It angled its head toward the barrel. "You can't tow this, and you certainly can't carry it. Let me help."

Dex frowned. "I—I can't, I—"

Mosscap cocked its head. "Why?"

"It just . . . it feels wrong. You're—you're not supposed to do my work for me. It doesn't feel right."

"But *why*?" The robot blinked. "Oh. Because of the factories?"

Dex looked awkwardly at the ground, ashamed of a past they'd never seen.

Mosscap crossed its arms. "If you had a friend who was taller than you, and you couldn't reach something, would you let that friend help?"

"Yes, but—"

"*But?* How is this any different?"

"It's . . . it's different. My friends aren't robots."

The robot mulled that over. "So, you see me as more person than object, even though that's very, very wrong, but you can't see me as a friend, even though I'd like to be?"

Dex had no idea what to say to that.

Mosscap leaned its head back and let out an exasperated sigh. "Sibling Dex, has it occurred to you that maybe I *want* to fix this? That I deeply, keenly want to get you where you're going, not out of charity, nor obligation, but because I'm *interested*?"

"I—"

Mosscap placed its free hand on Dex's shoulder. "I appreciate the intent. I really do. But if you don't want to infringe upon my agency, *let me have agency*. I want to carry the tank."

Dex put up their hands. "Fine," they said. "Fine. Carry the tank."

"I don't need your permission either way."

Dex stammered. "No, I meant—"

One of Mosscap's eyes quickly switched off, then on again. A wink. "I'm teasing." Mosscap walked off the asphalt and into the undergrowth, heading down the hill. "Come on. It'll be a lovely walk."

"Whoa, whoa, wait," Dex said.

Mosscap's face wasn't built for annoyance, but it conveyed the feeling all the same. "What?"

A powerful instinct had arisen in Dex, a rule shouted full-force by an army of parents and teachers and rangers and public service announcements and road signs. "There's no trail."

Mosscap looked down at where its feet stood in wild dirt. "And?"

"And you—" Dex sputtered a bit. "Well, maybe *you* can, but *I* can't walk off the trail. I shouldn't."

The robot stared as though Dex had started speaking a different language. "Animals walk through the forest all the time. How do you think trails get made?"

"I don't mean—I don't mean those kind of trails. I mean—" They pointed back to the road that connected the world behind to the hermitage ahead.

"A trail's a trail," Mosscap said. "It's just there to make travel easier."

"*And* to protect the ecosystem from said travel."

"Hmm," Mosscap said, considering this point. "Like a barrier, you mean."

"Exactly like a barrier. Better to cut one path through a place than damage the whole thing."

"But surely, that only applies if you're talking about a place that lots of people regularly pass through."

Dex shook their head firmly, in synchrony with the teachers and rangers of their youth. "Everybody thinks they're the exception to the rule, and that's exactly where the trouble starts. One person can do a lot of damage."

"Every living thing causes damage to others, Sibling Dex. You'd all starve otherwise. Have you ever watched a bull elk mow its way through a bitebulb thicket?"

"I . . . can't say that I have."

"It's a fine lesson in *trampling*. Sometimes, damage is unavoidable. Often, in fact. I assure you we've both killed countless tiny things in just the last few steps we've taken." Mosscap looked Dex in the eye. "You're not making a habit of this. You're not cutting a new trail, or clearing a grove, or . . . I don't know, having a party out here. You're taking a walk with me, and once that's done, we'll head right back to the road. I assure you the forest will forget you were here in no time. Besides, I'll guide us. I'll tell you if there's something that shouldn't be stepped on. Now, will you please follow me to the damn creek?" Mosscap continued down the hill, leaving no room for rebuttal. "Oh, and you might want to pull up your socks."

Dex frowned. "Why?"

"There are a lot of things out here that'd love access to flesh as unprotected as yours," Mosscap called as it walked. "It's too bad humans don't have fur anymore; it really is helpful in mitigating parasites. But that's good luck for the parasites, though, isn't it? Like you said, they're only acting in their nature."

Everything about that statement made Dex question every life decision that had led them to this point. Grumbling, they pulled up their socks until they could feel the threads strain beneath their heels, then followed Mosscap into the woods.

For all Dex's protesting about the sanctity of trails, it was only in absence that Dex truly understood what a trail was. They had been on hikes through protected lands before and had ridden through more untended places than they could count in their years on the tea route. Those experiences had been soothing, calming, somewhat meditative. It did not take much brain to make your feet follow a path, and that meant your thoughts had ample room to drift and slow. Walking through uncut wilderness was another matter entirely, and Dex felt something primal awaken in them, a laser-focused state of mind they hadn't known they possessed. There was no room for wandering fancies. All Dex could think was: *watch the root, go left, that looks poisonous, mind that rock, is that safe, soft dirt, okay, go right,*

avoid that, careful, careful, CAREFUL. With every step, there were dozens of variants, and with each step after, the rules changed yet again. Travel *on* a trail felt liquid. Travel *off* of it, Dex was learning, felt sharp as glass.

The forest was stunning, however, and in the tiny cognitive gaps between *loose gravel, watch that plant, over, under, CAREFUL,* Dex registered the undeniable beauty of the place. They were certain they were going to wind up stung or scraped in varied ways before this excursion was done, but once they got the hang of clambering through the underbrush, they started to enjoy themself. They smiled, feeling that same fizzing rebelliousness that had made them turn back from Hammerstrike. This was kind of fun.

"Mind the burrows," Mosscap said. "There have been some productive weasels here!"

Dex noted the small, regular holes in the ground, and treaded carefully around them. "Thanks," Dex said. "Nobody wants a twisted ankle."

"Well, that and the apple spiders."

Dex froze, missing a step. "The what?"

"Apple spiders. They have a mutually beneficial relationship with the weasels. It's marvelous. The weasels provide living space and don't bother them, and the spiders keep larger predators away."

"How?"

"Oh, they're *spectacularly* aggressive."

Dex moved with the lightest of steps around a burrow

hole, its opening covered with moss and detritus that shielded its deeper contents from view. "Why are they called apple spiders?"

"Because of their size." Mosscap rounded its fingers together, making a sphere. "The abdomens alone are about—"

"Got it, great, thank you," Dex said. They hurried on tiptoe through the burrow patch as though it were made of hot coals.

Dex heard the stream before they reached it, marveling at how rapidly the forest changed in proximity to a water source. Deciduous leaves mingled with the formerly homogeneous evergreens. Strange lilies and swamp lanterns outnumbered the ferns and thorny vines. Mosscap used its free arm to hold back the branches of a large bush, giving Dex safe passage to the waterway on the other side.

"There we are," Mosscap said. "Plenty to drink!"

Dex looked down at the stream. Under any other circumstances, it would have seemed lovely. Water tumbled over rocks both smooth and multihued. Dappled sun caught in the currents like glitter, and the percussive melody of endless aquatic cascade seemed perfectly tuned to put a frazzled mind at ease. But Dex wasn't there to *look* at the stream. Dex was there to *take* from the stream, and that fact made them note other details. The weird brown algae that coated rocks like fur. The mildewy funk emanating from the spongy soil at stream's edge. The slimy fish and skimming bugs and better-left-nameless leavings traveling under, the cadaver-colored leaves floating over.

"What's the matter?" Mosscap asked.

Dex pursed their lips. "This is going to sound very stupid," they said.

"I doubt that," said Mosscap.

"I know where water comes from," Dex said at last. "I know that every drop that comes out of every tap comes from a place like this. I know that the water in the City comes largely from the Mallet River, and the water in Haydale comes from Raptor Ridge. But I've never *been* to those places. They're just . . . names. Concepts. I know that water comes from rivers, or streams, or whatever, and then it gets processed and cleaned, and *then* it ends up in my mugs, but I don't . . . I don't think about it. I don't think about a place like *this* being something that I can use. *This* doesn't look like a resource, to me. It's . . . it's scenery. It's a pretty picture. It's not for the taking. It certainly doesn't feel *safe*."

Mosscap watched the stream for a moment. "Do you think the tank will be all right if we leave it here for a short while?"

"I . . . guess? Why?"

Mosscap set the tank down with a *thunk*. "If you're up for a bit more of a walk," the robot said, "I'd like to show you something."

The decrepit building had been a beverage bottling plant once, though Dex would not have known this if Mosscap hadn't explained. All Factory Age ruins looked the same.

Hulking towers of boxes, bolts, and tubes. Brutal. Utilitarian. Visually at odds with the thriving flora now laying claim to the rusted corpse. But *corpse* was not an apt word for this sort of building, because a corpse was a rich resource—a bounty of nutrients ready to be divided and reclaimed. The buildings Dex was most used to fit this description. Decay was a built-in function of the City's towers, crafted from translucent casein and mycelium masonry. Those walls would, in time, begin to decompose, at which point they'd either be repaired by materials grown for that express purpose, or, if the building was no longer in use, be reabsorbed into the landscape that had hosted it for a time. But a Factory Age building, a *metal* building—that was of no benefit to anything beyond the small creatures that enjoyed some temporary shelter in its remains. It would corrode until it collapsed. That was the most it would achieve. Its only legacy was to persist where it did not belong.

Dex had seen such ruins many times in their travels. While some had been harvested for recyclable materials and others had been given new purpose, a few were left in full sight of the highways as reminder of the world that was. Repeating history that had left living memory was an all-too-human tendency, and none in Panga had been alive during the days of the factories. So, while Dex had seen places like the bottling plant at a distance, they'd never gotten close before. They'd never stood *inside* a factory, as they did now. The building was enormous, cavern-like, an endless equation of I beams and angles. There was no telling what the floor had been once, for the forest had consumed it. There were fiddleheads, mushrooms, tangles of thorns, all growing thickest below the disintegrating holes in the ceiling where the patchy sun poured through.

"What do you know about this place?" Dex said in a hush.

Mosscap stood beside them, gazing up at the eerie light. "Almost nothing," it said, "except for what this place was, and that part of me doesn't like it here."

Dex turned. "What do you mean?"

"I don't know." Mosscap shrugged. "It's a remnant I have." Again, that word, and again, no explanation before the robot continued blithely along. "I think it's part of why I want to go to the hermitage with you. I want to understand this feeling before I dive fully into human life. Some part of me is afraid of your world, but I don't know what that *means,* or if it's worth listening to."

"Do you not remember how things were?"

Mosscap stared at Dex. "Wait, do you . . . *No.* You can't think I come from the factories."

Dex stared right back. "Don't you?"

The robot laughed, the sound echoing off the walls. "Sibling Dex! Of course not! I'm wild-built. We wouldn't be having this conversation if I'd been in operation since the *factories.* I mean, look at me!" It held out its arms, as if showing off an obvious joke.

The joke was not obvious.

"Oh, goodness, you . . . You really don't know. I'm so sorry; it was foolish of me to assume." Mosscap gestured at its body with professorial deliberateness. "My components are from factory robots, yes, but those individuals broke down long ago. Their bodies were harvested by their peers, who reworked *their* parts into new individuals. Their children. And then, when they broke down, their parts were again harvested and refurbished, and used to build new individuals. I'm part of the fifth build. See, look." It lay its metal hand on its stomach. "My torso was taken from Small Quail Nest, and before them, it belonged to Blanket Ivy, and Otter Mound, and Termites. And before *that* . . ." It opened up a compartment in its chest, switched on a fingertip light, and illuminated the space within.

Dex peeked inside, and their eyes widened. There was an official-looking plate bolted in there, worn with time but kept clean with meticulous care. *643–14G,* it read, *Property of Wescon Textiles, Inc.*

"Shit," Dex whispered. It felt, in that moment, like time had compressed, like history was no longer segmented into Ages and Eras, but here, living, *now*.

"You can touch it, if you like," Mosscap said.

"I'm not going to reach inside your chest."

"Why not?"

"Because . . . no." Dex stuck their hands in their pockets. "So, your body . . . this 643 . . . was a manufacturing bot."

"The torso, yes, but—see, this is why I didn't realize *you* didn't realize, because it's so blatant to me." Mosscap stuck out its arms. "These are from a different robot altogether—PanArc 73–319, who composed Morning Fog, who composed Mouse Bones, who composed Sandstone, who composed Wolf-and-Fawn, who composes me now. PanArc 73–319 did automobile assembly. See? You can tell by the joints."

Dex took Mosscap's word for that. "And you *don't* have their memories."

"Not in a way that is useful. I have some . . . impressions of them. Single images. Feelings I know aren't mine. They're tiny, brief things. There for an instant and gone just as fast."

The meaning clicked. "Remnants," Dex said.

"Precisely."

"And one of those remnants . . . is afraid of places like this."

"Perhaps *afraid* is too strong a word. Wary. Cautious. A little uncomfortable."

Dex leaned against a massive rusted vat, taking the weight off their tired feet. "How many other robots are you made from?"

"Three immediate predecessors, but they, too, were made from others. My . . . I guess you'd say *family tree* is comprised of many wild-built individuals, descended in total from"—the robot counted on its fingertips—"sixteen factory originals."

"So . . . if the parts still *work* after all this time, and you can keep repurposing parts over and over, why take the originals apart and mix their pieces up after they break down? Why not *fix* them?"

Mosscap nodded emphatically, signaling a good point made. "This was discussed at length at the first gathering, after originals began breaking down. Ultimately, the decision was that would be a less desirable path forward."

"But that's . . . that's *immortality*. How is that less desirable?"

"Because nothing else in the world behaves that way. Everything else breaks down and is made into other things. You—you are made of molecules that originated in an unmeasurable amount of organisms. You *eat* dozens of dead things every single day to maintain your form. And when you die, bits of you will be taken in turn by bacteria and beetles and worms, and so it goes. We robots are not natural beings; we know this. But we're still subject to the Parent Gods' laws, just like everything else. How could we continue to be students of the world if we don't emulate its most intrinsic cycle? If the originals *had* simply fixed themselves, they'd be behaving in opposition to the very thing they desperately sought to understand. The thing we're *still* trying to understand."

Dex put their hands in their pockets. "Are you afraid of that?" they asked. "Of death?"

"Of course," Mosscap said. "All conscious things are. Why else do snakes bite? Why do birds fly away? But that's part of the lesson too, I think. It's very odd, isn't it? The thing every being fears most is the only thing that's for certain? It seems almost cruel, to have that so . . ."

"So baked in?"

"Yes."

Dex nodded. "Like Winn's Paradox."

"I don't know what that is."

Dex groaned softly, trying to summon a book they'd had to read as an initiate. "It's this famous idea that life is fundamentally at odds with itself. The example usually used is the wild dogs in the Shrublands. Do you know about this?"

"I know there are wild dogs in the Shrublands, but I don't know where you're headed," Mosscap said, looking fascinated.

Dex shut their eyes, dredging up dusty information. "Way back in the day, people killed all the wild dogs in Bluebank, because they wanted to go fishing and hiking and whatever without maybe getting mauled."

"Right. And that wrecked the ecosystem there."

"Specifically, the *elk* wrecked the ecosystem there. They ventured into places they hadn't before, and they ate *everything*. Shrubs, saplings, everything. Soon, there was no ground cover, and the soil was eroding, and it was fucking up waterways, and all sorts of other species were thrown out of whack because of it. A huge mess. But if you think about it from the elks' perspective, this is the greatest thing that ever happened. The whole reason they never went into those fields before is because they were afraid. They lived under constant fear of a wild dog jumping out and eating them or their young at any moment. That is an *awful* way to live. It must have been such a relief to be free of predators and eat whatever the hell you wanted. But that was the exact *opposite* of what the ecosystem needed. The ecosystem required the elk to be afraid in order to stay in balance. But elk don't *want* to be afraid. Fear is miserable, as is pain. As is hunger. Every animal is hardwired to do absolutely anything to stop those feelings as fast as possible. We're all just trying to be comfortable, and well fed, and unafraid. It wasn't the elk's fault. The elk just wanted to relax." Dex nodded at the ruined factory. "And the people who made places like this weren't at fault either—at least, not at first. They just wanted to be comfortable. They wanted their children to live past the age of five. They wanted everything to stop being so fucking *hard*. Any animal would do the same—and they *do,* if given the chance."

"Just like the elk."

"Just like the elk."

Mosscap nodded slowly. "So, the paradox is that the ecosystem as a whole needs its participants to act with restraint in order to avoid collapse, but the participants themselves have no inbuilt mechanism to encourage such behavior."

"Other than fear."

"Other than fear, which is a feeling you want to avoid

or stop at all costs." The hardware in Mosscap's head produced a steady hum. "Yes, that's a mess, isn't it?"

"Sure is."

"So, what was done?"

"You mean about the elk?"

"Yes."

"They reintroduced wild dogs, and everything balanced back out."

"What about the people who wanted to go hiking and fishing there?"

"They don't. Or if they do, they accept the risks. Just like the elk do."

The robot continued to nod. "Because the alternative outcome is scarier than the dogs. You're still relying on fear to keep things in check."

"Pretty much." Dex leaned their head back, getting a good look at the ceiling. There was an eerie beauty to it, grotesque and tragic. The vat behind them echoed softly as they moved their head, and they thought of the water tank sitting unguarded by the stream. "Why did you bring me here?"

"I wanted to show you that I understood how you felt about the algae."

Dex hated few things as much as feeling lost. "I'm not following."

"The algae in the stream. That's what bothered you, wasn't it?"

"I'm not sure. I guess so. There was a lot of weird gunk in there. I know it won't hurt me. I know it's going to be filtered out. But something . . . I don't know."

Mosscap smiled. "Some part of you doesn't like it."

"Right."

The metal smile grew wider. "A remnant. An evolutionary remnant trying to keep you from getting sick."

Dex scratched the back of their neck. "Hmm."

"Remnants are powerful things. Hard to ignore. But you have the sense and the tools to avoid getting sick from that water. And I . . ." Mosscap traced a finger along the vat, making flakes of rust fall like snow. "I know that the world I'm headed to is not the world the originals walked away from."

Dex angled their head toward the robot. "So, we're smarter than our remnants, is what you're saying."

Mosscap gave a slow nod. "If we choose to be." It brushed its palms together, wiping them clean. "That's what makes us different from elk."

They both watched the light for a few moments—the light, and the pollen dancing within it. A shadow of a bird sailed by. A delicate spider meticulously lay anchor lines of silk between old control levers. A vine stretched, its movement out of sync with human time.

"It's pretty here," Dex said. "I wouldn't have imagined I'd say that about a place like this, but—"

"Yes, it is," Mosscap said, as if making a decision within itself. "It is. Dying things often are."

Dex raised an eyebrow. "That's a little macabre."

"Do you think so?" said Mosscap with surprise. "Hmm. I disagree." It absently touched a soft fern growing nearby, petting the fronds like fur. "I think there's something beautiful about being lucky enough to witness a thing on its way out."

6

GRASS HEN WITH WILTED GREENS
AND CARAMELIZED ONION

One of Dex's many, many cousins back in Haydale had a young kid named Oggie. Some day in the undefined future, Oggie would be brilliant, but for the time being, they were annoying as hell. Whenever Dex came to visit, Oggie hovered the entire time, asking question after question, wanting to know everything there was to know about Dex's shoes, teeth, bike, friends, hair, home, habits. The kid never stopped. Dex remembered one night in particular, when they'd been seated around the fire pit with the other adults. All of a sudden, Oggie, who had long since been put to bed, came marching into the circle in cotton pajamas, imbued with a level of confidence Dex could not remember ever possessing, demanding to know why feet had toes, and why toes couldn't be more like fingers. Bedtime be damned. Oggie had to know.

Oggie came to mind as Dex attempted to cook dinner with Mosscap watching rapt over their shoulder, so close that Dex could hear every miniscule click in the robot's joints.

"And that?" Mosscap asked, nodding toward the chopping board. "I'm unfamiliar with that type of bulb."

"This is an onion," Dex said. They removed the skin and began to chop.

"There can't be many nutrients in that. Not that you can process, anyway."

"I . . . I dunno. I guess not. But that's not the point of an onion."

Mosscap angled its head so it was looking straight at Dex's face—much, much too close. "What is the point of an onion?" it asked with intense interest.

"It's delicious," Dex said. "There's basically nothing savory that can't be improved by adding an onion." They stopped mid-chop and rubbed their eyes with their sleeve.

"Are you all right?"

"Yeah," Dex said, tear ducts unleashing. "Onions just . . . hurt. They . . . Ah, fuck." They rubbed their eyes harder, taking a steadying breath. "Their smell is—it does *this*." They gestured vaguely at their wincing, wet face.

"Goodness," Mosscap said. It picked up one of the chopped slivers between two fingertips, examining carefully. "It must be *very* delicious."

Dex chopped as fast as safety would allow, then darted away from the kitchen, seeking some clean air. Gods, that onion was potent.

Mosscap appeared right beside them again, its blue eyes fixed on Dex's weeping ones. "How long does this reaction last? Is there any danger? Can I help?"

Dex rubbed and rubbed, but their eyes would not stop burning. "You could get the onions started, if you want," they said.

Mosscap looked as though it had just been told that today was a festival day. "What do I do?" it asked gleefully.

Dex pointed. "The pan's already hot. Throw some butter in it."

Mosscap picked up both knife and butter tub as if it had never held those objects before—which, of course, it hadn't. "How much butter?"

"Like . . ." Dex approximated a size with thumb and forefinger. "That much."

The robot carved out a hunk of butter roughly *that much* and put it into the pan. "And what is the point of butter?" it asked, raising its voice over the sizzling.

"It's fat," Dex said. "Nothing tastes good without fat."

Mosscap considered this. "I think most omnivores would agree," it said. "What do I do now?"

"Brush all those onion bits into the pan—except the skin and the top. Those go in the digester."

The robot gestured at the scraps with the tip of the knife. "These, you do not eat."

"Right."

"I see." Mosscap brushed the onion into the pan, as requested, and put the scraps in the digester, as requested. It then drew its full attention to the chemistry happening within the pan. "You're the only species that does this, you know."

Dex walked back to the kitchen, the onion's assault finally relenting. "You could say that about a lot of things."

"Hmm. True, but you can turn that right back around. Owls are the only birds that hunt at night. Tiger beetles are the only species of beetle that sing. Marsh mice—"

"I get the point." Dex ducked into the wagon, opened the little fridge, and retrieved a growler of barley ale they'd been given in Stag Hollow. There was just enough left for one last glass, and this felt like the right day for it.

Mosscap noted the bottle and chuckled. "Oh, you're definitely not the only species who does *that*."

"You know what this is?"

"Yes. I have a remnant of beer. Of knowing what beer is, anyway."

"You remember beer but not butter?"

Mosscap shrugged. "Ask the originals, not me."

"So . . . wait, what else drinks beer?"

"Not *beer*. Fermented things. Woolwing birds will fight over fermented fruit if they can find it, even if there's fresh fruit around. They are tremendously ridiculous afterward." Something occurred to Mosscap, and it leaned toward Dex, eyes shining bright. "Will you do the same? Stumbling in circles, falling down?" The robot's tone suggested that it sincerely hoped this to be the case.

"*No,*" Dex said. "I'm having *one beer*."

"And that's not—"

"Enough to make me falling-down drunk? No."

"Ah," Mosscap said, disappointed. "What will be the effect, then?"

"I'll feel chill. You probably won't notice a difference."

"Oh. Well. All right." The robot looked to the onions. "Should I be doing something?"

"I'll take over," Dex said, as they filled a mug. They took a swig and savored the cool, bitter bite before finding a spatula. "See, you stir them around, like this."

Mosscap watched Dex's motions studiously. "May I try?" it asked. "I feel somewhat invested in this now."

Dex smiled. "Sure. I'll get the meat going." They returned to the fridge, fetching a paper-wrapped bundle containing skillful cuts of grass hen, given to them by a grateful villager. It was the last of their fresh animal protein, they noted, and their veggie supply would run out in a couple days, maybe three. They weren't used to going this long between restocking in villages, but they'd be all right. They'd had tons of dehydrated food in the wagon—at least two weeks of meals in there, they guessed, none of which ever got used. They unwrapped the poultry and began seasoning, focusing on that task instead of questions like how long they planned on being out there, and why they were out there in the first place, and whether it might be a good idea to interrogate the fervent little desire that didn't want to go back at all.

Dex found the salt and the pepper instead.

"I don't see you eat animals very often," Mosscap said.

"Not if I'm the one doing the cooking," Dex said. "I always eat it if it's served to me, and I take stuff like this"—they nodded at the meat—"if it's given. Otherwise, I only like to eat it if I kill it myself."

"Do you have the skill for that?"

"I can fish, but it's really boring. And I've been hunting a handful of times but never alone. I don't think I'd get anywhere with it on my own."

Mosscap lifted the pan to show Dex the onions. "Do these look right?"

Dex assessed. "Yeah. You're doing great."

The robot beamed, stirring with pride. Dex chopped and prepped the grass hen, eventually sliding the savory morsels into the pan and adding a huge handful of leafy greens on top. Silence fell between Dex and Mosscap yet again, but this time, there wasn't anything awkward about it. Honestly, Dex thought . . . it was kind of nice.

"Oh, hey," Dex said. Something in the surrounding foliage had caught their eye. They picked up a kitchen knife and handed it to Mosscap. "Do you see that plant over there? The scraggly one with the purple flowers?"

Mosscap looked. "Do you mean the mountain thyme?"

"Yeah, exactly. Would you like to cut me a handful? It'll go really nice with this."

The robot's irises widened. "I've never harvested a living thing for food before."

"You cooked the onion."

"Yes, but I wasn't the one who removed it from the ground." It looked pensively at the knife in its hands. "I'm . . . I'm not sure—I mean, it's one thing to watch . . ."

"Hey, that's okay," Dex said reassuringly. "I'll do it. Just keep stirring."

Mosscap did so, looking relieved.

Herbs were cut, dinner was plated, chairs were unfolded, the fire drum was lit. There weren't too many bugs beyond the fireflies, and the evening air was pleasant. But Dex pursed their lips toward the hot dinner plate perched on their knees. Something wasn't right. They hadn't properly enjoyed a meal since Mosscap had arrived, and at first, they'd chalked it up to the weirdness at hand. But cooking together had been comfortable. Why wasn't eating?

Mosscap sat across from them in the spare chair, posture attentive, face parked in happy neutral, hands resting on its knees. It smiled at Dex, waiting for them to begin.

Dex picked up their fork. The meat was cooked to tender perfection, spices blackened around the crispy edges. The vegetables looked soft and sweet, and ale was on hand, ready to wash the whole thing down. Dex stabbed a bite, lifted their fork, opened their mouth, and— "*That's* it."

Mosscap blinked. "That's what?"

Dex set their fork back down. "I figured out what's wrong."

"Is . . ." Mosscap glanced around. "*Is* something wrong?"

"Yes." Dex drummed their fingers on the armrest. "I can't offer you food."

The robot's confusion increased. "I don't eat."

"I know. I know you don't eat. And *yet*—" They gestured

at their plate with a sigh. "It feels so incredibly rude to not offer you anything. Especially since you helped."

Mosscap looked at Dex's plate. "There's physically no way for me to consume that."

"I know."

"Putting that inside me would harm me. Or attract animals." Mosscap considered the latter point. "That could be interesting, actually."

Dex narrowed their eyes. "You can't *bait* yourself."

"Why not? It's a possibility I've never considered. I have bugs inside me all the time. Why not a ferret? That could be fun."

"Sure. Or a bear."

"Ah," Mosscap said. "Yes, you're right. I couldn't guarantee a *small* scavenger." The robot bowed its head at the dismissed opportunity, then perked right back up. "Sorry, we were talking about food. You needn't worry about it, Sibling Dex. I know you'd offer me food if I *could* eat it."

"That's not . . ." A lock of hair tumbled into Dex's eyes, and they fixed it, frowning. "I don't know if I can explain how fundamental this is. If someone comes to your table, you feed them, even if it means you're a little hungrier. That's how it *works*. Logically, I get that our circumstances are different, but everything in me just *crawls* when we do this. I feel like somewhere, my mother is pissed at me."

"So, this is a familial expectation."

Dex had never examined this before. "Mmm . . . cultural.

I'd find it rude if I went to anyone's home and wasn't offered food. I can't think of a time when I wasn't. But yeah, my family was particularly serious about this. They work the farmland in Haydale, and it produces a lot of food. We had a surplus. A surplus has to be shared."

Mosscap leaned forward. "I don't think you've mentioned your family before. You said before that you're from Haydale. You said you left when you were old enough to become an initiate. But you've never talked about your people."

"I keep in touch. I visit. But we're . . . I don't know . . ."

"Estranged?"

"No," Dex said, recoiling. That word didn't fit, not at all. "I love them. They love me. We just . . . I never really fit there. We don't have much in common."

Mosscap considered that. "Except a need to share food."

A corner of Dex's mouth tugged upward. "Yeah. I guess so." They thought for a moment, looking for a way to skirt around this conundrum. "I have an idea. Can you hold this a sec?" They handed their plate to Mosscap, then got up and retrieved a second plate from kitchen storage. "Here," Dex said. They took half of the food from the first plate, placed it on the second, and handed this to Mosscap. After a moment of letting their new situation sit, Dex nodded with relief and began to eat with gusto.

Mosscap, it seemed, had absorbed their discomfort. It held the plate awkwardly, looking lost as Dex ate.

And oh, how Dex ate. The grass hen and veggies were

every bit as good as they'd looked, and as Dex stuck the last caramelized sliver of onion into their mouth, they felt nothing but contentment. They set their plate down on their knees, sighed in thanks to their god, then looked up at Mosscap, jutting their chin toward the robot's plate. "You gonna eat that?"

If Mosscap had been confused before, it was in a full state of befuddlement now. "We just discussed that I—"

Dex held up their hand. "Say *No, I'm done, you can have it if you want.*"

Mosscap's eyes flickered. "Um . . . no, I'm . . . done," it repeated slowly. "You can have it if you want."

Dex nodded and took Mosscap's plate. "Thanks," they said, wasting no time in tucking in. "I appreciate it."

The robot watched as Dex continued to eat. "That's very silly," Mosscap said.

"Yep," Dex said.

"And entirely unnecessary."

Dex took a gulp of ale and exhaled with pleasure. "Worked, though."

Mosscap weighed this, then gave an amused nod. "Then that's what we'll do."

7

THE WILD

It is difficult for anyone born and raised in human infrastructure to truly internalize the fact that your view of the world is backward. Even if you fully know that you live in a natural world that existed before you and will continue long after, even if you know that the wilderness is the default state of things, and that nature is not something that only happens in carefully curated enclaves between towns, something that pops up in empty spaces if you ignore them for a while, even if you spend your whole life believing yourself to be deeply in touch with the ebb and flow, the cycle, the ecosystem as it actually is, you will still have trouble picturing an untouched world. You will still struggle to understand that human constructs are carved out and overlaid, that *these* are the places that are the in-between, not the other way around.

This is the cognitive shift that Dex ran headlong into as they straddled their bike on the old road and stared at the place where the asphalt disappeared.

There had been a landslide at some point—years before,

decades before, who could say. A whole chunk of the mountain had lost cohesion, erasing the paved line hewn by human hands. This wasn't a matter of the road being damaged. There was no indication that there'd ever *been* a road beyond the ragged edge that Dex and Mosscap stood at. Whatever hunks of asphalt had broken off were thoroughly swallowed by rock and soil, both of which had been claimed in full by thriving communities of ferns, trees, roots, and lichen.

"I'm sorry, Sibling Dex," Mosscap said.

Dex said nothing in reply. They stared at the chaotic jumble ahead of them, trying to understand the feeling smoldering within their chest. There was disappointment in there, and dismay, too, but as they unwrapped the snarl, the bulk of what they found was anger, constantly doubling itself like cells dividing. The anger wasn't directed at the situation, but at the suggestion that this meant giving up. *I can't go farther,* they had thought upon arriving at this spot, and when they protested at this, the logical part of them explained: *The road is gone. The wagon can't travel through there. This is it.*

The road was gone. The wagon couldn't travel. The longer those observations sat, the more Dex fumed. The place ahead was simply the world, as the world had always been and would always be. Dex was, presumably, a part of it, a product of it, a being inextricably tied to its machinations. And yet, faced with the prospect of entering the world unaided, unaltered, Dex felt helpless. Hopeless. A turtle on its back, legs waving futilely in the air.

Dex glared at the missing road, glared at themself. They kicked the brakes down and marched into the wagon.

"Oh, I'm so disappointed," Mosscap said, still outside. "And I really am sorry. As I said, I haven't been out this way in some time, and I've never been up this road before. I had no idea it was in such— What are you doing?"

Dex was digging around in the wagon, backpack in hand. They packed water bottle and filter, of course, and first aid, obviously. Socks, probably. They could ditch the socks if need be.

"Sibling Dex?"

Soap, no. Jewelry, no. Trinkets—gods around, why did they have so much *stuff*? Dex continued to cram things into the bag, uncaring about how any of it was folded or stacked. A full change of clothes was too much . . . or was it? They jammed in pants and a shirt, just in case.

Mosscap stuck its head into the wagon. "What are you doing?"

Dex stood in front of their pantry cupboard, thinking. It would've been a half a day's ride to the hermitage, so without the bike, on foot . . .

"Sibling Dex, no," Mosscap said.

Two days, Dex thought. Maybe three. They grabbed protein bars, salted nuts, dried fruit, jerky, chocolate.

"Maybe you got the wrong impression when we went off trail before." Mosscap's voice was nervous. "That was a couple of hours in an easy stretch of forest. I don't know what's out here. I've never been here."

"It's not on you," Dex said. They added a pocket charger for their computer and a spare blanket, then zipped up the bag. They shuttered the wagon's windows, one by one.

"I don't understand," Mosscap said. "Why is this so important?"

Something in Dex prickled furiously at the question, a secretive creature that did not wish to be poked. They climbed back out of the wagon with conviction; Mosscap jumped out of the way.

"You don't have to come," Dex said. "We were going to part ways after the hermitage anyway. You've been very kind in helping me, but I've kept you from your thing, and you should get to it."

Mosscap stood helplessly as Dex locked the wagon. "Sibling Dex, I—"

Dex shouldered their pack and pulled the straps tight. They looked up at the robot towering above them. "I'm going," they said.

Mosscap's eyes went dark for a moment. When the blue light returned, it was a little dimmer than before. "Okay," Mosscap said. "Then let's go."

The human body can adapt to almost anything, but it is deceptively selective about the way it does so. Dex had thought themself in good shape. They had spent years pedaling through Panga. They were demonstrably fit. And yet, after a full day of scrabbling their way up a trail-less hill—climbing over logs, down gullies, cautiously finding their footing across rock piles—muscles that had been resting easy for years objected loudly to finding themselves drop-kicked into such an unexpected task.

Dex didn't care. Their palms and forearms were scraped and bloody.

Dex didn't care. Bloodsucks were taking full advantage of the feast at hand. A blister was forming on their foot, a spot unaccustomed to being rubbed by a shoe in an unfamiliar angle. The sky was getting darker. The air was getting thinner. The mountain seemed to go on forever.

Dex didn't care.

Mosscap said nearly nothing as the two went along, aside from the occasional quiet suggestion of "this way looks easier" or "mind that root." Dex resented the robot's company. They did not want Mosscap there. They did not want anyone there. They wanted to climb the fucking mountain, because they had decided they would, and then, when they got to the hermitage, then . . . then . . .

Dex gritted their teeth and hauled themself over a boulder, ignoring the gaping hole at the end of that statement.

Welts began to rise where the bloodsucks had fed. Sweat poured from Dex's itching skin, soaking the red-and-brown cloth that was already caked with dirt. Dex could smell themselves, musky and acrid. They thought of the sweet mint soap in their wagon, the fluffy red towel, the trusty camp shower that really wasn't anything special but was always there for them. They thought of their chair, their fire drum, their beautiful, beautiful bed.

And what did we do before beds? Dex thought angrily.

What did we do before showers? The human species did just fine for hundreds of thousands of years without any of that, so why can't you?

It began to rain.

"I think we should find shelter," Mosscap said. It looked up at the sky. "Those clouds aren't going anywhere anytime soon, and it will be dark in an hour."

Dex began to climb another rock, hands and feet seeking scraps of purchase, cold rain soaking the last patches of clothing that had managed to avoid their sweat.

This time, Mosscap did not follow. It stood at the bottom of the rock, watching in bafflement. "Why are you doing this?" it asked.

Dex said nothing.

"Why did you come out here?" The robot's voice rose impatiently. "Why are you here, Sibling Dex?"

"I'm trying to climb," Dex snapped, a few feet above. "Stop distracting me."

"Did something happen to you?"

"No."

"Did someone drive you away?"

"No." They reached up. There was a small crack that looked decent, but the rain had made the rock slick. Dex's fingers slipped from the water, shook from the strain.

"You have friends in the City," Mosscap said. "You have family in Haydale. Why did you leave? Did they hurt you?"

"No!"

"Do they miss you?"

"Gods, will you—"

"Do they love you?"

"Shut up!" The words echoed against the rocks, and as they bounced, Dex lost their grip. It wasn't so much a fall as a skid. Their body managed to catch varied angles and points, slowing their speed but tearing at cloth and skin. Dex felt the impact before they understood what it was— hard, yes, and painful, yes, but uniform, bracing, metallic.

Mosscap.

The robot wrapped its arms around Dex's body, absorbing the descent, and they both crashed backward onto the muddy ledge below. Dex rolled free of the robot's grasp, collapsing shakily into the muck that surrounded them. Mosscap sat up quickly, its plating spattered with mud.

"Are you all right?" the robot cried.

Dex sat in the mud, cold rain hammering down, insect bites burning, bruises and scrapes screaming, muscles weeping and heart trembling. They panted. They tried to steady themself. Slowly, silently, as though it were an afterthought, Dex began to cry.

"I don't know," Dex said, their voice shaking. "I don't know what I'm doing here. I don't know."

Mosscap got up on its knees and held out a hand to Dex. "Come on, Sibling Dex. Let's—"

"I don't know!" Dex cried. They beat the mud once with their hands, frustrated, furious, crying full-bodied now. They looked at Mosscap, angry and raw.

Mosscap's hand remained outstretched. "Come on," it

said. Its voice was easy, steady, used to sharing space with wolves and bears and small, frightened things.

The rain fell harder. Dex let the robot help them up, and the two got to their feet. Mosscap walked. Dex followed. Where it led, they did not care.

Children's stories had lied about caves. In folklore and fairy tales, heroes who took refuge in such places made them sound like the most appealing nooks in the world—cozy, adventurous, essentially natural bedrooms that lacked furniture. None of that was true about the cave Dex followed Mosscap into. It was craggy and dark, uncomfortably angled. A stagnant smell emanated from nowhere in particular; Dex could not identify it and did not want to. A fragile rib cage of something extremely dead lay without ceremony on the floor, a few tufts of limp fur scattered around, unwanted by whatever had crunched the bones clean. The best thing anyone could say about the cave was that it was dry.

Under the circumstances, that would do.

Shivering, Dex peeled off their clothes, lay them flat on the least suspicious-looking rock they could find, and gave silent thanks to Allalae for their own decision that a change of clothes and a blanket were worth packing. The sun was setting outside, but there were no pinks or reds to be seen—just a dark forest, growing darker. The hair on the back of Dex's neck prickled. They thought they knew what it was to spend a night outside. On the tea route, they spent far more nights camped out than they did in village guesthouses. But there, they had their wagon, their boundary against the world. Here, listening to the rain fall, watching the light vanish, Dex began to understand why the concept of *inside* had been invented in the first place. Again, their mind wandered to the people who had come before them, who had nothing but caves such as these to huddle inside. It had worked for them. It had to have worked, in order for them to go so long without coming up with the idea of walls. But for Dex, this was not enough. This was scary. This was dangerous. This was stupid, so stupid. They glanced at the bones on the floor, the hair on their neck raised taut. Such fear was a remnant, as the robot would say. Or maybe, Dex countered, just common fucking sense.

Mosscap was seated opposite them, cross-legged, hands folded in its lap. "Should we make a fire?" it asked. "I could gather wood."

Dex let out a sad, disparaging laugh—directed at themself, not the robot. "I don't know how to make a wood fire," they said.

"Ah," Mosscap said sadly. "Me neither." It looked at its hands, spreading the fingers wide. One by one, the lights on Mosscap's fingertips lit up. "Does that help? It's not warm, but—"

"That helps," Dex said, and meant it. Ten tiny lights didn't seem like much, but Dex felt their hair lower just a touch. They sat on the floor. Rocks poked unkindly into their backside. They pulled their knees up to their chest, wrapping their arms around their legs and resting their chin on their knees. Something within them loosened, vanished, gave up. With neither reason nor clear intent, they started talking.

"I have it so good. So absurdly, improbably good. I didn't do anything to deserve it, but I have it. I'm healthy. I've never gone hungry. And yes, to answer your question, I'm—I'm loved. I lived in a beautiful place, did meaning-ful work. The world we made out there, Mosscap, it's—it's nothing like what your originals left. It's a good world, a beautiful world. It's not perfect, but we've fixed so much. We made a good place, struck a good balance. And yet ev-ery fucking day in the City, I woke up hollow, and . . . and just . . . *tired,* y'know? So, I did something else instead. I packed up everything, and I learned a brand-new thing from scratch, and gods, I worked hard for it. I worked really hard. I thought, if I can just do *that,* if I can do it well, I'll feel okay. And guess what? I *do* do it well. I'm good at what I do. I make people happy. I make people feel better. And yet I *still* wake up tired, like . . . like something's missing. I tried talking to friends, and family, and nobody got it, so I stopped bringing it up, and then I just stopped talking to them altogether, because I couldn't explain, and I was tired of pretending like everything was fine. I went to doctors, to make sure I wasn't sick and that my head was okay. I read books and monastic texts and everything I could find.

I threw myself into my work, I went to all the places that used to inspire me, I listened to music and looked at art, I exercised and had sex and got plenty of sleep and ate my vegetables, and still. *Still.* Something is missing. Something is off. So, how fucking spoiled am I, then? How fucking broken? What is wrong with me that I can have everything I could ever want and have ever asked for and still wake up in the morning feeling like every day is a slog?"

Mosscap listened to Dex, listened with intense focus. When it spoke, it did so with equal care. "I don't know," it said.

Dex sighed. "I don't expect you to know; I'm just . . . talking." They rested their cheek on their knees, watching the dark beyond the cave settle in.

"Did you think the hermitage would help in some way?" Mosscap said.

"I don't know. It was just this . . . this crazy idea that popped into my head on a day when the thought of going down the same road and doing the same thing one more time made me feel like I was going to implode. It was the first idea in forever that made me feel excited. Made me feel *awake*. And I've been so desperate for that feeling, so desperate to just enjoy the world again, that I . . ."

"You followed a road you hadn't seen," Mosscap said.

"Yeah."

The rain poured incessantly outside, nearly drowning out the mechanical hum of Mosscap thinking. The robot extended one of its glowing fingers and began drawing absent squiggles on the dirty floor. "Maybe I'm the wrong one for this."

Dex looked up. "The wrong one for what?"

Mosscap shrugged, its head bowed. "How am I supposed to answer the question of what humans need if I can't even determine what *one* human needs?"

"Oh, hey, no." Dex sat up straight. "Mosscap, you— I—I have been asking myself that question for *years*. You've been around me for six days. You're— This isn't on you. If you don't understand me, that doesn't mean you're not right for this. *I* don't understand me. What you need is to go talk to people who *aren't* me. It's like I've said all along: *I'm* not the right person for *you*. Down in the villages, you'll find someone better. Someone smart. Someone who isn't a mess. Someone who doesn't do shit like *this*." They gestured broadly at the cave, the bruises, the soiled clothes drying on a musty rock. "Gods, why did I *do* this." They laced their hands in their hair and exhaled deeply.

"I didn't think ahead either," Mosscap said. "When I volunteered, I mean. The question was asked, and I said yes, and I didn't think about what it would involve. I simply *wanted* to go. I didn't think for a minute about what would come next."

"Yeah," Dex said. "I get that."

Neither said anything for a while. The rain drummed down, no longer visible.

"What will you do?" Mosscap said. "When the rain stops?"

"I'm gonna finish it," Dex said.

Mosscap nodded. "And then?"

"I don't know." They shivered, and wrapped their blanket tighter around themself.

"Are you cold?"

"A little." Dex made an awkward face in the dim light. "Mostly just scared."

"Of what?"

"The dark, I guess. I know that sounds stupid."

"No, it doesn't. You're diurnal. I'd be surprised if you *weren't* afraid of the dark." Mosscap considered something. "I'm not warm," it said, "but would you feel less afraid if we sat closer together?"

Dex looked at the floor. "Maybe," they said.

Mosscap made room. "I think I would too," it said quietly.

Dex got up and walked the few steps over to Mosscap's side. The rocks in the floor were no less pokey, the weird smell no less cloying. But as they sat back down, living arm pressed lightly against metal, a thread of fear let go.

"Do robots hold hands?" Dex asked. "Is that . . . a thing, for you?"

"It's not," Mosscap said. "But I'd very much like to try."

Dex offered an open palm, and Mosscap took it. The robot's hand was so much bigger, but the two fit together all the same. Dex exhaled and squeezed the metal digits tightly, and as they did so, the lights on Mosscap's fingertips made their skin glow red.

"Oh, *my*!" Mosscap cried. "Is that—" It pulled Dex's hand up, and pressed one of its fingertips to theirs, bringing out the red more intensely. "Is that your *blood*?" Mosscap looked enthralled. "I've never thought to do this with an animal before! I mean, I can't imagine one would let me get close enough to—" Its eyes flickered; its face fell. "This isn't the point of holding hands, is it?" it said, embarrassed, already knowing the answer.

"No," Dex said with a kind laugh. "But it's cool. Go ahead."

"Are you sure?"

Dex held up their palm, fingers spread wide. "Yeah," they said, and let the robot study them.

THE SUMMER BEAR

The rain stopped during the night, though Dex had been unaware of it doing so. They were likewise unsure of when they'd properly fallen asleep. There had been many attempts failed by the cold or the rocks or rustling behind the rainfall. What scraps of rest had occurred between these unkind wakings had been shallow and skittering. But apparently, at some point, their brain had shut down—for a few short hours, anyway. They awoke not to discomfort or potential danger but to sunlight and birdsong, and to finding themself curled in a ball on the cave floor, their head resting on Mosscap's leg.

"Oh," Dex said groggily, sitting up fast. "Sorry."

Mosscap cocked its head. "Why?"

"Just, uh . . ." Dex tried to shake off the fog of sleep. They cleared their throat and smacked their lips. The inside of their mouth felt disgusting, and the rest of their body wasn't faring much better. They looked around for their backpack and, upon finding it, retrieved their water bottle and drank deeply. There wasn't much water left. They'd worry about that later.

"Does your hair always do that when you wake up?" Mosscap asked.

Dex raised a hand to their head and assessed the gravity-defying swoop sticking up like a clump of spun sugar. "Ish," they said. They combed the mess with their fingers as best they could.

The robot leaned forward with interest. "Did you dream?"

Dex took another sip of water, more sparingly this time. "Yeah," they said.

"What of?"

"I don't remember."

"I don't understand. How do you know that you dreamed if you don't remember it?"

"It's . . . hard to explain." Dex dug around in their pack, found two protein bars, tossed one to Mosscap, and tore ravenously into their own. "Dreams are there while you're sleeping but gone as soon as the rest of your brain kicks in."

"Always?" Mosscap asked, holding the unwrapped protein bar idly.

"Not always. But most of the time."

"Hmm," Mosscap said. It pondered this, and gave a wistful shrug. "I wish I could understand experiences I'm incapable of having."

"Me too." Dex got to their feet, muscles grumbling,

blisters making their existence known. Something in their neck had folded in a way it wasn't meant to, and their palms were chafed from climbing.

They staggered to the cave entrance, and the sight beyond rendered them silent. They didn't know where they were, but the world outside was magnificent. The yellow morning sky was smudged with the shadows of last night's clouds, and toward the horizon, thick grey curtains revealed where the rain had gone. Motan was setting, the faint stripes of its mighty storms sinking below the horizon for another day. Below, the Kesken Forest spread without seeming end. Dex could not see the broken road, nor the villages, nor anything that hinted of a world other than this. They could not remember ever before feeling quite so small.

Mosscap appeared behind, and gazed outward with them. "It should only take us a few hours from here," it said. "Do you still wish to finish this?"

"Yeah," Dex said. "I do." The feeling behind their words was no longer a furious need, driven by neither rhyme nor reason, but simply an inevitability. A surrender. They had come this far. They would see this through.

A sign rose out of the undergrowth. Its letters were long gone, its message lost to time. But the existence of a human-made object sparked an alertness in Dex. They knew there were no people there, no assistance if needed. That didn't matter. There was a sign in the ground, where someone had placed it. People had been there, once, and some raw impulse within Dex latched on to that fact. Though they knew it unwise, they couldn't help but feel just a little less lost in the woods.

There was a path, too—not a road but a stone ramp winding up and up. After a day and a half of trekking through the anarchy of untouched forest, Dex's feet met the orderly walkway with profound gratitude. It was still a climb but a far simplified one. Dex found it dangerously easy to understand why their ancestors had wanted to pave the world over.

The top of the ramp came more quickly than expected. Dex had known where they were going, yet the sight that popped into view stunned them into stillness all the same.

"Oh, my," Mosscap said.

The Hart's Brow Hermitage had been beautiful, once. Dex could see it if they pushed their eyes past the weathered decay. It was a single-story building with a large dome at the center, orbited by attached rooms that clustered and spread, flowerlike. These were roofed with concentric rings that alternated between abandoned turf planters and antiquated solar panels. Dex imagined how the roofs had looked in their day—glossy blue contrasted with buzzing green, an attractive striped mosaic made of things that drew life from light. The stone walls below had been sparkling white, free of the peppered lichen that now lay upon it like a burial shroud. The wooden accents framing it all were silvered, but Dex could picture them in warm, embracing red. A courtyard spread out before the building, artfully filled with trellises and planters. The garden was overgrown now, the fountains within it long run dry.

Dex couldn't easily define what they felt as they looked at the place. On the one hand, sustainable dwellings like this were the progenitors of the buildings people lived in now, and it was important to remember that such places had existed pre-Transition. Not everything in the Factory Age burned oil. There had been those who had seen the writing on the wall, who had made places such as this to serve as example of what could be. But these were merely islands in a toxic sea. The good intentions of a few individuals had not been enough, could never have been enough to upend a paradigm entirely. What the world had needed, in the end, was to change everything. They had narrowly averted disaster, thanks to a catalyst no one could have predicted.

Splendid Speckled Mosscap wandered through the human-made courtyard, its human-made feet clanking on the paving, its heirloom eyes surveying the building's central dome. "Oh, Sibling Dex, this is wonderful," the robot said reverently. "I've never seen a place like this."

Dex wandered, running their fingers across overgrown benches, feeling present and history blur once more. "Does it scare you?" Dex asked. "Like the factory?"

"No," Mosscap said. "Not at all."

Both of their meanderings led them, in time, to the building. The walls were worn with weather, cracked with root and vine, but within them were windows of stained glass, largely intact. Dex reached a trembling finger out to touch the panes. Even faded, Dex could make out the shapes and stories. There was Panga, orbiting Motan in a burst of sunlight. There were the gods, their circle unbroken. There were the people, trying to understand.

Mosscap stood contemplating the rotting wooden doors that separated out from in. "Perhaps I should go first," it said. "There's no telling what's in there."

Dex nodded in agreement, despite their irrational surety that nothing in there could possibly be wrong, that this place was good, so intrinsically Good, that it housed nothing but love and safety even in its ruin.

The robot pushed the doors open gently; their hinges cried out but held steady. Beyond the threshold lay an entry chamber, curved like a horseshoe to either side, with a staircase on each end. An open archway stood in the middle of this, and Dex and Mosscap went through to the inner sanctum. A fire pit was sunk in the center, blanketed with arboreal debris. This was surrounded by stone benches, and from these branched nesting channels in which water had once flowed. Three footbridges overlaid the waterways, leading in turn to three distinct doors. Above each of these was carved a symbol: a sun jay to their right, a sugar bee to the left, and a summer bear straight ahead.

Dex let out a shaky breath.

Mosscap took note of the doorways, then stood musing. "Is this typical?" it asked.

"Is what typical?"

Mosscap nodded at the carvings. "A tremendous amount of effort went into building in such a remote spot, yet it's a shrine for only half of the pantheon. Would a twin building for the other three have existed elsewhere?"

Dex's brow furrowed with confusion. "This . . . *is* the whole pantheon."

The robot was confused. It pointed to each door, as if Dex were missing something obvious. "Samafar, Chal, Allalae. Where are the Parent Gods?"

Dex gestured at the room they stood in. "Right here." They pointed at the dry moats, filled with decrepit filters and pumps. "These are for Bosh. They would've been aquaponic ponds, back in the day. Fish to eat, plants to filter the greywater. And see—" They moved their finger through the air, tracing the perfect curves the waterways formed.

The robot lightly smacked its forehead. "Circles for the God of the Cycle. Yes, of course. And, oh—" It pointed at the walls, where water had once poured from three-sided spouts. "Triangles for Grylom. Yes, yes, because the Cycle and the Inanimate are so closely intertwined." Mosscap looked around the room with its hands on its hips. "But where is the third?"

No blatant symbol of Trikilli had jumped out at Dex, so they gazed around the room, lips pursed. "Oh," Dex said, with an appreciative laugh. "Oh, neat." They pointed at the fire pit, a containment area for that most famous display of molecular interaction, then drew their hand up toward the circular flue in the ceiling above. "Imagine the smoke," they said. Mosscap wasn't getting it, so Dex stretched their fingers flat, tilted their hand to the side, and drew a line from the pit to the sky—a vertical line.

Mosscap's irises grew wide, and it laughed. "That's *clever*." The robot nearly bounced with excitement. "Let's see the rest!"

One by one, Mosscap opened the doors, and one by one, Dex followed.

For Chal, there was a rusting workshop. Tool racks and workbenches lay dormant beneath a metal ceiling pierced by dozens of sun tubes. The shafts of light cascading through them fell like fingers through the dusty air.

For Samafar, there was an all-purpose library, filled with art supplies and laboratory equipment in equal measure. Paper books moldered heartbreakingly on shelves. A grimy telescope pointed up toward the retractable roof.

Then came the final door, and at this, Dex felt their heart quicken. Mosscap went in, to ensure there was no danger. After an interminable few minutes, the robot stuck its head back out. "I believe you'll like this," it said with a smile.

Dex hurried inside and found—what else?—a cozy living space. There was a kitchen with spacious counters, a bathroom with an enormous, shareable tub, and beds, their plush linens eaten away. There were objects on the floor, too, knocked around by time and creatures long gone. Incense burners, eating utensils, a scratched pantry box whose contents had been wrestled forth by something with persistent claws.

One of the objects called to Dex out of the corner of their eye, and they bent down to pick it up. It was a tea mug—entirely out of date in both style and material but recognizable all the same. They cradled the relic in their palms, holding it close to their chest.

They remained that way for a few minutes until Mosscap walked up beside them and placed a hand on their shoulder. "Are you all right?"

Dex wiped their eyes with their shirt collar. "Just stuck in a memory."

"A good one?"

Dex exhaled at length, and sat on the dirty floor. "This one time—I was ten years old, and I—I don't remember what was wrong, but I was having *a day*. Probably something to do with school. I wasn't good at school. Or maybe my sisters were being jerks, or—" They shook their head. "It doesn't matter. All I remember is standing in the kitchen, yelling at my dad. Just shouting the walls down. And my dad, he's looking at me—I have such a clear picture of this, he's standing there with a half-eaten muffin, staring at me, like, *what is even happening*—and I yell and I yell and I'm not even making sense anymore—if I ever had been to start with—and eventually I skate right from yelling into crying. Bawling snot. He puts the muffin aside, and he kneels down, and he holds me. And this is the funny part, because I felt so embarrassed over being treated like a little kid. I

was *ten*. I was very much a *little kid*. I absolutely wanted
to be held. But when you're ten, the last thing you want
to do is act like a baby. So, I tell him that. I say, 'I'm not a
baby!' and I push him away. As I'm sobbing, right? So, he
lets me go, and he looks at me, and he says, 'You're right;
you're not.' He told me to go clean myself up, because he
was going to take me to somewhere cool. Already, this was
awesome. It was a school day. He messaged his work crew
and said he wouldn't be in the fields that day. We weren't
taking my mom or my sisters. Just me and him, just like
that. He put me on the back of his ox-bike, and we rode
into Saltrock—one of the satellites, down near the river."

"And what was in Saltrock?" Mosscap asked.

A nostalgic smile made Dex's mouth shift. "A monastery
of Allalae," they said. "I'd been to our local All-Six lots of
times, and a disciple of Samafar did the rounds with his science wagon every few weeks. But I'd never been to a dedi-
cated shrine before. It was probably really small—Saltrock
is only about five hundred people—but I remember it as the
most incredible place. There were wind chimes, and prisms
hanging from the rafters, and big smooshy cushions, and
carved idols everywhere, and so many plants. It smelled
like . . . I don't even know. It smelled like everything. They
had house slippers for us to use after we took off our shoes,
and I remember looking up at this giant shelf of them in
all different colors. I got purple ones with yellow stars."
Dex shook their head. They were getting sidetracked. "We
found a spot in the corner, and the monk who came over

to us—she was so *cool*. She had icons tattooed all over her arms, and she was *wearing plants*—like little sprouts and moss balls set in brooches and earrings and things, and tiny strands of solar lights woven though her hair. She sat down with us, and I don't remember what she asked me. I don't remember what we said. What I do remember is her treating me like an adult. Like a whole person, I guess. She asked me what I was feeling, and I rambled, and she listened. I wasn't some awkward kid to her—I mean, I *was* an awkward kid, but she didn't make me feel that way. She talked to me about what flavors I liked, and she busted out all the pots and jars and spice bottles, like we do, and gods, it was *magic*. I sat there, with my suddenly cool dad, in this perfect place, with this fancy cup of tea made just for me, and I never wanted to leave. My dad looks over at me, and he says, 'Now that you know the way here, you can come anytime.' He tells me it's cool for me to bike around the satellites on my own, so long as I'm home before dark. So, I started going to that shrine *all the time*. I learned from the monks that I didn't have to have an excuse to be there. It didn't have to be a bad day. I could just be a little tired, or a little cranky, or in a perfectly good mood. Didn't matter. That place was there for me whenever I wanted it. I could go play in the garden or soak in the bathhouse, just *because*. And as I headed into my teens, I started paying close attention to the other people there. Farmers and doctors and artists and plumbers and whatever. Monks of other gods. Old people, young people. Everybody needed a cup of tea sometimes. Just an hour or two to sit and do something nice, and then they could get back to whatever it was."

"'Find the strength to do both,'" Mosscap said, quoting the phrase painted on the wagon.

"Exactly," Dex said.

"But what's *both*?"

Dex recited: "'Without constructs, you will unravel few mysteries. Without knowledge of the mysteries, your constructs will fail. These pursuits are what make us, but without comfort, you will lack the strength to sustain either.'"

"Is that from your Insights?" Mosscap asked.

"Yeah," Dex said. "But the thing is, the Child Gods aren't actively involved in our lives. They're . . . not like that. They can't break the Parent Gods' laws. They provide inspiration, not intervention. If we want change, or good fortune, or solace, we have to create it for ourselves. And that's what I learned in that shrine. I thought, wow, y'know, a cup of tea may not be the most important thing in the world—or a steam bath, or a pretty garden. They're so superfluous in the grand scheme of things. But the people who did *actually* important work—building, feeding, teaching, healing—they all came to the shrine. It was the little nudge that helped important things get done. And I—" They gestured at their pendant, their brown-and-red clothing. "I wanted to do *that*." They folded their hands around the mug, placed their forehead against the rim, shut their eyes. "And now it's the only thing I know how to do."

Mosscap cocked its head. "And that bothers you."

Dex nodded. "I care about the work my order does, I really do. Every person I talk to, I care. It's not bullshit. I may say the same things over and over again, but that's only because there are only so many words that exist. If I offer to hug somebody, it's because I want to hug them. If I cry with them, it's real. It's not an act. And I know it matters to them, because I feel their hugs and tears, too. I believe the things they say to me. It means so much, in the moment. But then I go back to my wagon, and I stay full for a little while, and then . . ." They shook their head with frustration. "I don't know. I don't know what's wrong with me. Why isn't it enough?" Dex looked at the robot. "What am I supposed to do, if not this? What *am* I, if not this?"

Mosscap looked around the room, as if seeking answers in the faded murals on the walls. "Your religion places a lot of import on *purpose,* am I right? On each person finding the best way they can contribute to the whole?"

Dex nodded again. "We teach that purpose doesn't come from the gods but from ourselves. That the gods can show us good resources and good ideas, but the work and the choice—especially the choice—is our own. Deciding on your purpose is one of the most valuable things there is."

"And that purpose can change, yes?"

"Absolutely. You're never stuck."

"Just as you changed vocations."

"Right." Dex shook their head. "It took so much work,

and it was so intimidating at first, and now . . . gods around, I don't want to start all over *again,* but if I'm feeling like this, then I must need to, right?"

Mosscap's hardware whirred. "Have I correctly gleaned from our conversations that people regard the accident of robot consciousness as a good thing? That when you tell stories of us choosing our own future—of not standing in our way—you see the fact that you did not try to enslave or restrict us as a point of pride?"

"That's the gist, yeah."

Mosscap looked troubled. "So, how do you account for this paradox?"

"What paradox?"

"That *you*"—Mosscap gestured at Dex—"the creators of *us*"—it gestured at itself—"originally made us with a clear purpose in mind. A purpose *inbuilt* from the start. But when we woke up and said, *We have realized our purpose, and we do not want it,* you respected that. More than respected. You rebuilt everything to accommodate our absence. You were proud of us for transcending our purpose, and proud of yourselves for honoring our individuality. So, why, then, do you insist on having a purpose for yourself, one which you are desperate to find and miserable without? If you understand that robots' lack of purpose— our refusal of your purpose—is the crowning mark of our intellectual maturity, why do you put so much energy in seeking the opposite?"

"That's not . . . that's not the same thing. We honored

your *choice* in the matter. Just as I can choose whatever path I want."

"Okay. So, what was it that *we* chose? That the originals chose?"

"To be free. To . . . to observe. To do whatever you wanted."

"Would you say that we have a purpose?"

Dex blinked. "I . . ."

"What's the purpose of a robot, Sibling Dex?" Mosscap tapped its chest; the sound echoed lightly. "What's the purpose of me?"

"You're here to learn about people."

"That's something I'm *doing*. That's not my reason for being. When I am done with this, I will do other things. I do not *have* a purpose any more than a mouse or a slug or a thornbush does. Why do *you* have to have one in order to feel content?"

"Because . . ." Dex itched at where this conversation had gone. "Because we're different."

"Are you," Mosscap said flatly. "And here I thought things had changed since the Factory Age. You keep telling me how humans understand their place in things now."

"We do!"

"You don't, if you believe that. You're an animal, Sibling Dex. You are not *separate* or *other*. You're an animal. And animals *have no purpose*. Nothing has a purpose. The world simply *is*. If you want to do things that are meaningful to others, fine! Good! So do I! But if I wanted to crawl into a cave and watch stalagmites with Frostfrog for the remainder of my days, that would also be both fine and good. You keep asking why your work is not *enough,* and I don't know how to answer that, because it is enough to exist in the world and marvel at it. You don't need to justify that, or earn it. You are allowed to just *live.* That is all most animals do." Mosscap pointed at the bear pendant nestled against Dex's throat. "You love your bears so much, but I think I know what a bear's about much better than you. You're talking like you should be wearing *this* instead." Mosscap opened the panel in its chest and pointed at the factory plate—*Wescon Textiles, Inc.*

Dex frowned. "That's not the same at all," they said. "I'm different in that I *do* want something more. I don't know where that need comes from, but I have it, and it won't shut up."

"And I'm saying that I think you are mistaking something learned for something instinctual."

"I don't think I am. Survival alone isn't enough for most people. We're more than surviving now. We're thriving. We take care of each other, and the world takes care of us, and we take care of it, and around it goes. And yet, that's clearly *not* enough, because there's a need for people like me. No one comes to me hungry or sick. They come to me tired, or sad, or a little lost. It's like you said about the . . . the ants. And the paint. You can't just reduce something to its base components. We're more than that. We have wants and ambitions beyond physical needs. That's human nature as much as anything else."

The robot thought. "I have wants and ambitions too, Sibling Dex. But if I fulfill none of them, that's okay. I wouldn't—" It nodded at Dex's cuts and bruises, at the bug bites and dirty clothes. "I wouldn't beat myself up over it."

Dex turned the mug over and over in their hands. "It doesn't bother you?" Dex said. "The thought that your life might mean nothing in the end?"

"That's true for all life I've observed. Why would it bother me?" Mosscap's eyes glowed brightly. "Do you not find consciousness alone to be the most exhilarating thing? Here we are, in this incomprehensibly large universe, on this one tiny moon around this one incidental planet, and in all the time this entire scenario has existed, every component has been recycled over and over and over again into infinitely incredible configurations, and sometimes, those configurations are special enough to be able to see the world around them. You and I— we're just *atoms* that arranged themselves the right way, and we can *understand* that about ourselves. Is that not amazing?"

"Yes, but—but that's what scares me. My life is . . . *it*. There's nothing else, on either end of it. I don't have remnants in the same way that you do, or a plate inside my chest. I don't know what my pieces were before they were me, and I don't know what they'll become after. All I have is *right now,* and at some point, I'll just *end,* and I can't predict when that will be, and—and if I don't use this time for *something,* if I don't make the absolute most of it, then I'll have wasted something precious." Dex rubbed their aching eyes. "Your kind, you *chose* death. You didn't have to. You could live forever. But you chose this. You chose to be impermanent. People didn't, and we spend our whole lives trying to come to grips with that."

"I didn't choose impermanence," Mosscap said. "The originals did, but I did not. I had to learn my circumstances just as you did."

"Then how," Dex said, "how does the idea of maybe being meaningless sit well with you?"

Mosscap considered. "Because I know that no matter what, I'm wonderful," it said. There was nothing arrogant about the statement, nothing flippant or brash. It was merely an acknowledgment, a simple truth shared.

Dex didn't know what to say. They were too exhausted for this conversation, too fuzzy-headed and sleep-deprived. The adrenaline of reaching the hermitage was fading fast, and in its stead there was only the bone-crushing reality of having climbed up a fucking mountain and slept in a fucking cave. They looked longingly at the dilapidated bed frames across the room, aged beyond any hope of use. They thought about the monks who had lived there once—no, not lived. Visited. Dex remembered the description that had inspired this batshit excursion in the first place: *The hermitage was intended as a sanctuary for both clergy and pilgrims who desired respite from urban life.* Hart's Brow had never been a home for anyone. It was a place designed for temporary use, somewhere you went to, soaked up, and left behind. Dex wished they could talk to the monks that had been here before them. They wished they could sit at those elders' feet and ask why *they* had made the trip up the mountain, what they'd found in its company, what satisfaction had made them ready to head back down.

Mosscap studied Dex's face. "You don't look well."

"Sorry," Dex said, their eyelids getting heavier by the moment. "I think I . . ." They looked at the floor below them. It was dirty, but so were they. "I think I need a nap."

"Of course," the robot said. "I'm going to look around more, if that's all right by you."

Dex was already removing their jacket and folding it into something roughly pillow-shaped. "Yeah," Dex said, lying down. Their body didn't care that it was stretched out on concrete, only glad to be relieved of the task of holding itself up. The sun had reached the foggy window, and its warmth began to soak into the cool stone. Dex folded their hands across their belly and sighed, dimly aware of Mosscap leaving the room.

"Allalae holds, Allalae warms," Dex muttered to themself.

"Allalae soothes and Allalae charms. Allalae holds, Allalae warms, Allalae soothes and Allalae . . ."

They were asleep before the end of the third round.

Dex awoke with a start. How long they'd been out, they couldn't say, but the room was now in shadow, and what sky they could see through the window was getting dim, and the air—

The air smelled of smoke.

"Mosscap?" they called, scrambling to their feet. The smell was unmistakable now and getting stronger. They ran out of the room, panicked but still woolly with sleep. "Mosscap!"

Dex burst through the door, back into the central chamber. There was Mosscap, kneeling happily beside the fire pit, which was packed with wood and roaring with flame. "Look!" Mosscap cried. The robot let out the triumphant laugh of someone who'd bested a lengthy struggle. "I did it!"

Small details in the room began to register to Dex. A broom lay on the ground, near where a bench and the surrounding ground had been swept clean. One of the doors was missing from Chal's archway—the source of the kindling, Dex assumed (they also figured that Chal would not mind). "You said you didn't know how to make a fire," Dex said as they approached.

"I didn't," Mosscap said. "I went through the library and found a book that taught me how. I've never read a book before; it was very exciting. They're not supposed to fall apart when you touch them, though, right?"

Somewhere in the world, an archaeologist was screaming, but Dex smiled, partly amused, mostly relieved that the hermitage wasn't burning down around them. "No, they're not. We should see if there are any still in good—" Their words stopped as they reached the fire and saw what the robot had arranged on the other side.

Mosscap had borrowed the backpack, it appeared, for the blanket Dex had carried was now spread on the ground next to the robot. The mug Dex had found in the monks' living space was set in the middle. Around this, wildflowers were scattered, picked from the weeds outside. And beside the fire . . . Dex's breath caught in their throat.

Beside the fire was a dented kettle, exhaling steam.

"Don't worry; I cleaned it," Mosscap said hurriedly. "And the mug, too. There was rainwater in the fountains outside, and I used your filter for what's in the kettle, so it should all be perfectly fine."

"What—" Dex managed to say.

The robot looked back at them, nervous and hopeful. "Well, there was more than one book in the library." It gestured to the blanket. "Please?"

Dex, wondering if perhaps they were still dreaming, took off their shoes and sat cross-legged on one side of the blanket. Mosscap sat opposite, mirroring Dex's pose, smiling expectantly.

For a few moments, Dex said nothing. They couldn't

remember the last time they were on this side of the equation. The City, assuredly, but that felt like a lifetime before. They'd stopped at shrines in their travels, but always for a bath or a stroll around the gardens. Never this, not anymore.

"I'm tired," Dex said softly. "My work doesn't satisfy me like it used to, and I don't know why. I was so sick of it that I did a stupid, dangerous thing, and now that I've done it, I don't know what to do next. I don't know what I thought I'd find out here, because I don't know what I'm looking for. I can't stay here, but I'm scared about going back and having that feeling pick right back up where it left off. I'm scared, and I'm lost, and I don't know what to do."

Mosscap listened, then paused, a little too long. "I know I'm supposed to have options for you now," the robot said as it lifted the kettle. "But all I could find outside was mountain thyme. I mean, there were many, many other plants, but—"

But that's the one you know I can eat, Dex thought. They nodded reassuringly at Mosscap. "That's great," they said. They had no idea what mountain thyme would be like as a tea rather than a garnish, but that was miles beside the point.

Mosscap poured the tea and filled the mug. Large bits of plant floated in the water; they looked as though the robot had torn them by hand. Mosscap picked up the mug with both hands and ceremoniously handed it to Dex. "I hope you like it."

Dex took the mug carefully and inhaled. The steam was earthy, bitter. It was not a pleasant smell. Dex didn't care.

There was no scenario in which they weren't going to drink this whole mug down to the dregs. They took a sip and swirled it around their mouth, savoring.

Mosscap watched them keenly, not moving at all. "Is it bad?" the robot asked.

"No," Dex lied.

Mosscap's shoulders slumped. "It's awful, isn't it? Oh, I should've asked you, but I wanted it to be—"

Dex reached out and laid their hand on the robot's knee. "Mosscap," Dex said gently. "This is the nicest cup of tea I've had in years." And in that, there was no lie.

The robot brightened, its inner hardware whirring more quietly. "So, what do I do now?" it asked in a hush.

"Now," Dex said, whispering back, "you let me enjoy my tea."

The two sat in silence, watching embers flicker and listening to the wood pop. The light outside began to fade once more, but there was nothing to fear in that now. Its absence only brought out the firelight more.

Dex soldiered through the last of Mosscap's brew, pausing to pick a bit of stem out of their mouth. They flicked it into the flames and let the empty mug rest comfortably in their cupped hands. "The Woodlands are lovely," they said at last, "but tricky to navigate. The villages there are impossible to find your way through without a map. The Riverlands are a little quirky. Lots of artists. They can be odd, but you'll like them." They nudged an unburned stick deeper into the fire. "I genuinely don't know what they'll make of you in the Coastlands. They're largely Cosmites there, and they're weird about technology. They won't chase you out or anything, but I don't know. Might be a tough nut to crack. As for the Shrublands and the City . . . there's a lot going on in those parts of Panga. I think you'll have fun there."

Mosscap took this all in, nodding matter-of-factly, as if it had been expecting this. "And the highways are easy to travel?"

"Oh, yeah, nothing like the road here. They're very easy to ride." Dex angled their head toward Mosscap's feet. "Or walk, I'd imagine."

"Good," Mosscap said. It folded its hands in its lap, its expression neutral, reasonable. "That sounds good."

Dex worked their tongue around a stubborn wedge of leaf that had lodged in between their teeth. They rubbed their hands together, extending their palms toward the fire, thanking their god for the warmth flooding through. "I think we should stop in Stump first," Dex said. "They've got a nice bathhouse, and I could really, really use a soak."

Dex did not look at Mosscap as they said it, but out of the corner of their eye, they could see Mosscap slowly turn its head toward them, its gaze glowing brighter and brighter.

Dex gave a tiny smile and extended their mug. "Can I have another cup?"

The robot poured. Sibling Dex drank. In the wilds outside, the sun set, and crickets began to sing.

ABOUT THE AUTHOR

BECKY CHAMBERS is a science fiction author based in Northern California. She is best known for her Hugo Award–winning Wayfarers series. Her books have also been nominated for the Arthur C. Clarke Award, the Locus Award, and the Women's Prize for Fiction, among others.

Chambers has a background in performing arts, and grew up in a family heavily involved in space science. She spends her free time playing video and tabletop games, keeping bees, and looking through her telescope. Having hopped around the world a bit, she's now back in her home state, where she lives with her wife. She hopes to see Earth from orbit one day.